MW00652262

A Sea of Past and Present

Nellie Brooks

Merpaper Press LLC

Edited by Karen Meeus Editing

Published by Merpaper Press LLC

CONTENTS

CHAPTER 1

B illie Donovan?" Ava closed the door of the rental car that had taken her from San Jose airport to Mendocino Cove. Smiling, she shaded her eyes against the sun of a golden July afternoon and waved.

Living in Seattle, she had missed the warm, golden light and mild temperatures of her childhood. A cozy rain day was the best thing in the world when she wanted a cup of tea, a hot bath, and a good book. But once the tea was drunk, the bath taken, and the book read, Ava's long, gray days often got lonely.

After all, tea and baths and books couldn't fix a failing marriage or coax home an absent husband.

But now Ava had finally taken the trip to Mendocino Cove she'd promised herself for so many years, and the sweet sun and fresh sea breeze stirred something long lost in her heart and soul.

Squinting at the silhouette of a female figure standing beside an adorable seaside cottage surrounded by flowers, Ava remembered deep in her bones how the gorgeous days of her childhood had followed each other like shimmering pearls on a seemingly endless necklace.

"Billie!" she called out again, sure now that it was her old childhood friend. "Hey!"

"Ava! You made it!" Billie turned, laughed, and threw open her arms as if she could hug Ava from a distance. "Welcome home!"

"Billie! It *is* you!" Ava ran—no matter that she was a dignified forty-five years old and had last seen her best childhood friend several decades ago—across the garden and into her friend's arms. "I *missed* you!"

Billie squeezed her tight. "Ava, you look exactly the same! I got a shock when I turned, and you stood there like some ghost of the past! I didn't hear the car come up the street."

"Let me see you." Ava stepped back so she could see her old friend better. "Oh, my. A grown woman and everything." She smiled. "Do a twirl."

Smiling back, Billie raised her arms and turned on the spot like a ballerina in a music box. "Verdict? Don't tell me I still look the same. I won't believe you."

"You don't. You are *beautiful*," Ava said delightedly. Billie didn't look like she was an awkward thirteen anymore. The braces had given way to a wide, generous smile. The lanky, long-limbered body had filled in all the right places, and her bright eyes and light biscuit tan made her seem to burst with health and energy. Ava laughed. "Your pimples are gone!"

"Hey! *I* never had pimples." Billie grinned and pushed her gardening hat out of her forehead. "*You* did."

"Well, I guess I replaced them with wrinkles," Ava said happily. "I'm so glad to be here, Billie."

Driving across the mountain range, Ava had wondered if it would feel strange to see Billie again—let alone stay with her. They hadn't seen each other for so long. Maybe they had both changed so much, it would feel awkward.

It was clear that Billie harbored no such fears. "Come on. You must be exhausted." Unceremoniously, she slung an arm around Ava's waist and pulled her along.

Ava couldn't open her eyes wide enough as they walked on a stone path that led through a jumble of flowers to Billie's picturesque cottage. As if flowers and a cottage weren't enough, behind them lay the Pacific Ocean, sparkling and glittering in the sun like an azure jewel.

"What a stunning view!" Ava exclaimed. "Hold on a moment. I have to stop and admire it."

Billie let go and took off her gardening hat. "Admire away. I live here and still fall in love with the coast every day."

"What a beautiful spot, Billie. I'm so glad you get to live here." Ava meant it. It was a joy to find her friend so well and happy.

Billie smiled. "Let's go in the backyard and sit down. I made coffee. Or do you want tea?" She led the way.

"Coffee is fine. Anything is fine."

"Have a seat. Give me a minute to wash my hands and bring out the tray." Billie went inside.

Ava sank into one of the comfortable gray wicker chairs that stood on the small blue stone patio. It was surrounded by a riot of marigolds and beach daisies, coral bells and bougainvillea and yellow roses. Where it ended, another short, paved path led to an oversized dock.

Billie hustled in and out of the house, bringing coffee and cake to the table.

"Oh, wow. Can I help you?" Ava said, her eyes widening.

"Almost done. Sit tight. I baked this morning, so it's all fresh."

Ava shook her head. "I honestly don't know why I ever left the cove."

"I can answer that one." Billie set a last plate of poppy seed cookies on the table. Then she pulled a pair of gardening gloves out of her back pocket and dropped them to the floor before she plopped into her own wicker chair. She tossed her head back and ran her hands through her short curls, raking them back.

"I'm listening." Ava smiled.

"You left to go to college." Billie grinned. "And then you married Bruno, who charmed you with all the fire of an Italian Forno Cupola."

"A *dome-shaped brick oven?*" Ava had to laugh at the description, but then she sighed. "Actually, that sounds about right." Over the years, Bruno had indeed turned from a lover into a brick.

She turned to admire the abundant flowers. "Billie, I love your marigolds!"

Ava didn't want to talk about her marriage and spoil the moment.

All through her drive over the vineyard-dotted mountains, her mind kept flashing back to when she and Bruno were first married.

They had rented a villa in Tuscany for their honeymoon. They spent their days kissing and eating and hiking through beautiful Italian vineyards. Their nights were spent in each other's arms, with the bedroom windows open so they could feel the soft night air on their skin while they talked about their lives and their plans for their future together.

Ava had talked about her writing, her Californian childhood, and her attempts to cook the perfect pasta. Bruno talked about his architecture studies and his parents and described the streets and trattorias of Florence, where they would go next.

But that was a long time ago. Now it was different.

Bricks didn't talk. They were silent and firm and spent the vast majority of their time where they belonged. Which, in Bruno's mind, didn't seem to be their home. *House*, not home. It hadn't felt like a home since Zoe left for college.

"The marigolds are dear to my heart," Billie said and straightened back up to survey the table. "They grow from seeds. Can you believe it? After buying flats for years, they finally decided to seed themselves out now. Feels like a miracle every year." Reaching, she lifted an opaque glass dome off a stand, revealing the luscious cake hiding below.

"You didn't have to go to all this effort," Ava protested.

Billie shook her head to show it had been no effort. "I enjoy baking a good cake. I figured you would be hungry when you got here, and it's too late for lunch and too early for dinner."

Ava blinked at the loaded table. It looked so inviting with its delicate white china and pretty cake forks, floral napkins and vase full of marigolds and baby's breath. But the centerpieces were the decadent pies and cream tortes.

"Billie, baking a good cake is the understatement of the century. These are gorgeous! Did you really make them all yourself?"

"I bake to relax, my dear. The recipes are the result of many, many years of relaxation." Busily, Billie poured coffee from a white percolator. It smelled of rich roasted beans, and Ava took a deep breath, enjoying the deep aroma that filled the air.

Then Billie picked up a silver cake cutter and pointed at a milky-green cake stand. "This one is a strawberry cream cake." She cut a piece and set it on an empty plate so Ava could see what the torte looked like inside.

"Oh. You have no idea how I regret not visiting you earlier. That looks delicious." The light and fluffy sponge cake was layered with strawberries and cream, topped with more whipped cream, fresh strawberries, and toasted slivered almonds.

"This one here is a chocolate mousse torte." Billie cut the next torte and added the slice to the sampler plate.

"Hmm." Ava couldn't remember the last time she had anything as sumptuous as melted dark chocolate folded into whipped cream, spread between cake layers, and topped with chocolate ganache, chocolate shavings, and a leaf of fresh mint.

All the time Bruno spent at his office dictating things to his twenty-something secretary, Ginny, had made Ava insecure about her weight and shape. It set her on a course of cucumbers and celery and water instead of pasta and provolone and wine. Eventually, she'd figured it couldn't be her weight that kept her husband away because Bruno didn't seem to notice when she lost it. But Ava's sad cucumber habit had stayed.

Maybe her life would have been different had she eaten more chocolate ganache.

"And this one is my personal favorite. My grandmother's pistachio torte." Billie added a third piece to the sampler plate.

"I've never had pistachio torte," Ava said.

Thinking of Bruno had sobered up her giddy excitement at the reunion. She tried to recover it. The moment was too precious not to enjoy. "Um. How do you make it, Billie?"

Billie glanced at her. "I like to grind pistachios by hand until I have just the right amount of crunch and flavor. Then I mix them with almond flour, sugar, and eggs, and I like to use a wooden spoon. Nothing metallic; I think the metal reacts with the eggs. It takes longer, but it tastes better. Then I bake it, cut layers, and fill them with whipped cream and more chopped pistachios. That's it. It's very easy once you get the hang of it. I don't even need a recipe anymore." Billie leaned forward earnestly. "I had to make three cream cakes, Ava."

"Why?" Ava smiled at the expression in her friend's eyes. "What dark secret am I going to hear now?"

CHAPTER 2

The dark secret is that I bought way too much cream and need to use it up. Do me a favor and eat all you can, yeah? What do you want for starters?"

"The pistachio sounds incredible, but I simply can't resist the chocolate torte," Ava said and picked up her plate. "Just a small piece, please. I'm trying to watch the ol' waistline."

"Bah, nonsense." Billie set a slice as big as the Continental Divide on Ava's plate. "If you want to shortchange your taste buds, you'll have to do it yourself."

"Whoa." Ava's outstretched arm sank under the weight.

Billie grinned. "Welcome back, my dear." She helped herself to a piece of the pistachio cake. "Go on. Try a bite. I promise you'll like it. You used to be a chocolate fiend as a kid, remember?"

Ava returned the grin. "I once got in trouble because I had found my mother's secret stash of chocolate eggs. They were meant for Easter, but I dragged them into my treehouse and ate every last one. Mom was pretty... Actually, she was mostly worried I'd be sick."

"I remember that." Billie laughed. "Your mom was so nice. Didn't she even buy more, so you still had some to search on Easter? My mom would have smacked my bottom and called it a day."

"She did get more." Ava laughed, but then she sighed. "I miss my mother so much. She passed away five years ago, and each year I miss her more."

Bruno had been made senior partner of the architecture firm the same year Mom died. He'd been busy before, but after stepping into the partner role, he all but vanished from Ava's life. She'd spilled her tears by herself; some for her mother, some for her marriage. The two people she used to be closest to were gone. Mom forever. But five years ago, she'd still held out hope for her marriage.

"I'm so sorry about your mom," Billie murmured. "I understand completely. Are you all right?"

Ava tried to smile. "Of course I am. Hey, tell me more about this gorgeous garden. I don't remember it from when your parents lived in the house."

"I did most of it." Billie started talking about the creation of the garden. It had taken years, and the help of many neighbors and friends.

Listening and nodding in the right places, Ava picked up her fork and sank it into the creamy confection. "Oh, Billie," she interrupted her old friend mid-sentence. "This just *melts* in my mouth. I *can't*." She ate another luscious bite.

Billie laughed. "I was hoping you'd have that reaction."

It felt naughty to eat something so rich and crea my... A little of the good kind of naughty, and a lot of the bad kind.

Ava swallowed and lowered her fork.

"What?" Billie looked up. "Don't tell me it's too chocolaty for you?"

"On the contrary. It's perfection itself." Ava shook her head. "I'm in love with it. It's the best thing I've eaten in years. But I'll blow up like a balloon if I eat all that. I'm not kidding."

"Aww. Have your cake, Ava. It's fine. We'll just take a nice, long walk along the bluff tonight. You'll burn those calories off before you know it."

Ava doubted a nice walk across the bluff would burn the calories from the decorative chocolate shavings, let alone the actual cake. She put a sliver of cake on her fork and ate it, trying not to roll her eyes ecstatically. "How do you stay so slim?"

"Like I said, I walk it off." Billie was finishing up her pistachio cream, leaving not a crumb on her plate. "This garden is my gym. And I run a small animal rescue."

Billie set down her fork, then expectantly wiggled her fingers as she surveyed the table for her next treat. "See the enclosures over there?" She nodded over Ava's shoulder.

Ava turned and looked. "Yes, who are those for? Do you have patients in them?" She turned back and also ate another bite. *So good!* And just one more...

"Right now they are empty, thank goodness. But I often have pelicans or cormorants or gulls and sometimes orphaned sea lions. They keep me busy with cleaning and feeding and whatnot. I often go fishing for their food too. My brother has a little boat, and we like to take it out."

"I love that," Ava said and finished her cake, leaving only a celebratory smudge of ganache on her plate. "Your brother Jon, right?"

Was it indecent to lick the fork? At her age, didn't women say they found themselves and did exactly as they pleased? Furtively, Ava scraped off the last of the ganache and quickly ate it too.

"Yes, Jon, that's right. He runs a vineyard with a winery tasting room. Oh, and he's dating Jenny. Do you remember our Jenny?"

Jenny! Ava had *adored* Jenny, with her blue eyes and sun-bleached hair and long, tan legs and, last but not least, her pipe-smoking grandmother, who told the best spooky story at the beach bonfires in the Forgotten Cove. "Of course I do," Ava said. "We were best friends until her mother got lost in the forest. I thought Jenny moved to Nantucket after the funeral?"

"She was there for a few years, and then she married and moved to Maine. But she came back recently and now lives with her daughter in the old family hotel at Beach and Forgotten."

"And Faye?" Billie, Jenny, Faye, and Ava had been inseparable as kids.

"Faye and I stuck around Mendocino Cove," Billie said cheerfully. "Somebody had to!"

Ava smiled. "Not exactly a terrible fate, either."

"I enjoyed every second of it. Try the macarons if you don't want so many calories," Billie advised and helped herself to a handful of the airy pastel cookies. "Jon made them." She popped one into her mouth.

Ava took a pink macaron. And then a lavender one. It was even better than the first, and suddenly, despite all the guilty chocolate and the cookies she'd already eaten, she felt ravenous. All she'd had that day was half a whole-wheat sandwich with cream cheese—*scrape it extra thin if you please could, Mr. Sandwich Ma*n—and a small salad with shrimp and lemon juice for lunch.

For what? For whom? She was healthy as a horse, and all that low-fat food and picking on crumbs was pure vanity, wasn't it? Wasn't it? She cleared her throat. "Actually, I think I'll try another piece, Billie. It's too good to play coy."

She lifted her plate, feeling like Oliver Twist asking for more porridge. "Hallelujah!" Billie picked up the cake server. "Which one do you fancy?"

And just like that, the discipline of Seattle-Ava's life crumbled into dust and was carried off by the merry little sea breeze that swayed the marigolds and whispered to the roses.

Ava ate every last crumb of a luscious slice of pistachio torte so delectable she had to blink actual tears out of her eyes. Then she ate a piece of the fluffiest, fruitiest strawberry torte ever to dance over anyone's palate and, for good measure, another lavender macaron. And one yellow one. And last, a blue one to see if it tasted different, which it did, so she tried the green one too, simply because the smooth, shiny surface and slightly crunchy exterior with the soft, chewy filling was too good to pass up.

When Ava was done, she fell back into her chair and stretched out her legs in the most unladylike manner. "That was the best dang food I ever had in my life, Billie. I'm not even embarrassed about eating so much."

"And why would you be?" Billie cheered her with her coffee cup. "How about I show you your room, and then we take that walk along the bluff?"

"It won't burn many calories."

"Who's talking about calories? The goal is to work up a new appetite. I have planned a nice dinner for us too."

"Fine." Ava put her hands on her belly. "I'm not sure I can walk right now. Give me a moment."

"All right." Unbothered, Billie leaned back and held her face in the sun. "That's fine. We'll just stay here."

A phone beeped. "Sorry. That's me." Billie patted her pockets and pulled her cell phone out. "It's Jenny and Faye." She looked up from the screen. "They want to know if there's any cake left over. I think they're really asking whether it's okay to join us. Or are you too tired? You've had a long trip."

Ava sat up and straightened the skirt of her black wrap dress. "Despite my best efforts, there is more than enough left. And I'd *love* to see them," she said.

"We were counting on that. Hi, Ava!" Faye—tan, with wavy brown hair that contrasted her big blue eyes—came walking around the corner of the house.

"Ava!" Jenny came shortly behind her friend, carrying another covered cake tray in her hands. "I can't believe it's you!"

"You didn't wait like we said you would," Billie remarked critically.

"We heard there was strawberry torte and didn't want you to eat everything by yourself," Faye countered and walked around the table to hug Ava. "Hey, honey. Long time no see."

"I know." Ava had a hard time keeping her tears back. How could she have allowed herself to feel lonely in Seattle for so long when she could have returned to Mendocino Cove and her friends?

"Hi, pumpkin!" Jenny laughed and pulled Ava unceremoniously into her arms. "Looks like everyone's back!"

"Don't tell me you brought more cake," Billie said. "What did you make, Jenny?"

"As usual, *I* made nothing. Everything I cook tastes like straw in water. But Jon sends this." Jenny set her tray down, and Billie opened it.

"It's a passion fruit tart," Faye said, and cut herself a large triangle of strawberry cream torte while Jenny pulled up more chairs and went to get plates and cake forks.

"Oh. I never tried that." Ava couldn't eat another bite. But whatever was breaking free in her still wanted to at least sample this latest delicacy.

"Try a piece," Jenny said, and before Ava could protest, she had a succulent slice on her plate. "It's a buttery shortbread crust," Jenny explained. "The filling is sweet and pretty tangy. It's made with passion fruit juice, sweetened condensed milk, and whipped cream. It's lovely."

It smelled light and airy and tropical. Against her better knowledge, Ava lifted her fork. She took a bite of the tart. Full as she was, the flavor exploded in her mouth.

Ava sipped her coffee and, very slowly and bite by bite, ate the rest of her slice as she listened to the girls.

There'd be no more salads with light proteins for Ava now. None of her friends needed to lose weight. Maybe a walk across the bluff really was the solution, or maybe it had to do with the reason their eyes were shining and their laughter came easily.

In the end, it didn't matter to anyone but herself what she did or how she looked now. Her marriage with Bruno was over. She had decided that while driving over the mountains.

The only question she had left was, would he notice she was gone?

CHAPTER 3

I need to call my aunt. It's been too long since I've heard from her. She said she would come to visit, but something's gone wrong." Jenny looked at her daughter, Audrey, who was sitting cross-legged on a beach towel beside her, reading a book.

Audrey slid her sunglasses down and looked over the brim at Jenny. "We kind of need her here, Mom. Why didn't you say anything before if you are worried she won't follow through?"

Jenny picked up her white, lacy sundress and pulled it on before she answered. "I don't know. Maybe because the feeling isn't new. I guess I didn't believe her in the first place when she said she wanted to come home."

"Why doesn't she?" Audrey took the sunscreen lotion and squirted a dollop on the back of her hand. "What could possibly be better than living in a majestic hotel in a gorgeous, perfectly private, cobalt-blue cove?"

"Either it's the memories, or she simply can't be bothered, Audrey." Jenny didn't want to talk about all the reasons Georgie would rather stay away. She had never told her kids in detail what had happened to their grandmother Willow. It was a terrible story, and it was enough that they had to hear the sad ending.

The death of her sister—Jenny's mom—had broken Aunt Georgie. She had never been the same afterward.

"If she doesn't come, you could bring up on the phone that I would still love to open the hotel back up for business, Mom," Audrey said gently. "Tell her I'm qualified. I have a degree in hotel management that's hot off the press, and I've fallen in love with our old family hotel." She picked up her shirt dress and slipped her arms in. "Can you do that?"

"I already did, and I can try again. But it would be better to ask her in person. She's a slippery customer," Jenny said vaguely.

"I realize that, Mom. But I do need a job," Audrey said. "I love this hotel, and I'd love to stay in Mendocino Cove. I'd love to stay with you."

Jenny looked at her daughter. "I'd love that too," she said and smiled. "Don't worry. My own job starts in two days. You can stay here as long as you like. We won't starve, that's for sure." Jenny's friends and neighbors liked to cook, and a constant stream of delicious foods made its way into the hotel.

"Thanks, Mom. I really do appreciate it." Smiling, Audrey stood and patted the sand off, then rolled up her towel. Then her face grew somber. "I can stay for a while on your dime—but we both know that eventually, I'll need to earn my own way."

"Or you could marry rich," Jenny suggested helpfully.

Audrey laughed. "Like whom? Don't answer—I don't want to hear it. Let's try calling your elusive aunt and hearing what she has to say for herself."

"How about Michael? He's the owner of the Mermaid Galley and only, oh, fifteen or so years older than you. He's a fine match."

"Mom! Stop. Eww. Besides, Michael is clearly in love with Hannah, his waitress."

"At this point, who knows what those two are up to? Michael might marry you to make Hannah jealous." Jenny bit her lip to keep from laughing out loud at the absurd scenario.

"Yeah, sure. Good. I'm done. Bye." Shaking her head, Audrey stalked off toward the hotel.

Jenny grinned and grabbed her own towel and the bottle of sun lotion to follow her daughter.

"All right, I'll call," she conceded when she joined Audrey in hanging the towels on the line she'd hung from the cedar near the patio. "I'll just wash up and change, and then I'll do it. But prepare yourself. She might not answer."

"Oh, I know. Nobody is flakier than Georgie." Audrey leaned over and kissed Jenny's cheek. "Thank you, Mom. I'd call her myself, but I don't think she'll answer the phone for me. See you in twenty minutes?"

Jenny nodded.

She didn't like Audrey thinking of Aunt Georgie as a flake. But of course, Audrey was correct. Aunt Georgie was a total flake. Completely unreliable. Even when Jenny had been barely old enough to qualify as a teenager, it had been Jenny who took care of Georgie. Not the other way around.

But the hotel and its contents belonged to Georgie. With one possible exception.

Last month, Jenny had found an armoire full of antique treasures. The women of the family had collected it over generations, to serve as a nest egg for their children and children's children. There had also been a hidden note written by Jenny's grandmother, Rosie.

The note said that the antiques in the armoire were to be Jenny's, since Georgie had enough money already. But the note was not a legally binding document, and Grandma had written nothing about the antiques in her will.

Because of this, Jenny needed to ask Georgie for the heirlooms. And Jenny had no idea what Georgie would say. Yes? No? Anything was possible. Her aunt was terribly materialistic, but she was also unpredictable.

"Okay," Jenny murmured to herself. "Ask whether she will come like she promised. And ask about the heirlooms. I can do it."

But first, she had to wash off the beach. The thought of calling Georgie and having an organized conversation was enough to make Jenny sweat. Already her sunscreen was running into her eyes in that insidious way that sunscreen had. It burned.

Trying not to rub, Jenny went inside. She crossed the beautiful living room of the old mansion and passed the walk-in fireplace, the parlor, dining room, and cozy kitchen on her way to the foyer. There, her grandfather's famous sea glass chandelier dappled the white walls in all the blues and greens of the ocean, and Jenny stayed for a moment to admire the dancing, twirling spots.

Then she climbed the sweeping staircase, walked along the upper corridor to her bedroom, and closed the door behind her.

Like all bedrooms in the empty hotel, this one had a generously sized ensuite bathroom. In it was a tall mirror, a marble sink with a wooden vanity, a toilet, a recessed linen cabinet, a plush green rug the color of young rhododendrons in spring, and a freestanding tub with a white waffle curtain on rings as golden as the tub's clawed feet.

Audrey had put a vase full of flowers on the countertop, and their sweet floral scent mingled with that of handmade lavender soap and the fresh sprig of eucalyptus Audrey tied every other day to her mother's shower head. The sun shone cheerfully through the large window that looked out at the sea. Its rays shattered into fractals where they hit the crystal flower vase so that the fragrant, aromatic air shimmered in all the colors of the rainbow.

Jenny undressed and turned the shower on, then stepped into the tub. She'd have liked to stay and take her time enjoying the shower, but instead, she quickly rinsed off salt and sand and washed the salt out of her hair.

Mendocino Cove was going through a drought. Long showers were not sustainable until it rained. Even short showers were not an everyday luxury. Luckily, they had all the cold glory of the Pacific Ocean to swim in—and plenty of washcloths.

Jenny toweled off, ran a brush through her shoulder-length blond hair, and put aloe on her face. When that was done, she went into her room and put on fresh underwear, shorts and a blouse and strappy leather sandals.

Then she tied the sheer curtains of the enormous four-poster bed to the posts and sat on the soft white duvet.

"Okay. Ask Georgie to come, ask for the heirlooms Grandma wanted me to have," Jenny whispered to herself. She picked up her cell phone and tapped the screen.

CHAPTER 4

"Yeees?"

"Hi, Aunt Georgie! It's Jenny."

"Oh, hiii, darling." Aunt Georgie had a habit of drawing out her vowels. "Why are you calling me?"

"I wanted to ask when you are coming," Jenny said. It was best to get straight to the point. "Remember that you said you would visit?"

"Oh, honey, did I say that?"

"Yes, Aunt Georgie, you said you missed Grandma, and that you wanted to come home. We are so excited! Can you tell me when you'll get here?" Jenny closed her eyes. This was never going to work out.

"Honey, darling, I just have no idea! I can't remember saying I would come home." She made a small sound Jenny couldn't read. "Did you know, my Fred has passed away."

"Oh, Georgie, I'm so sorry. You were very fond of him, weren't you?"

Fred was Georgie's fourth husband. Fifth? Jenny had lost track. Her aunt had a knack for finding rich old men who were happy to marry, happy to have fun, and happy to leave their merry wife a fortune.

But Fred had been different. He, too, had been wealthy and ready to squeeze the most fun out of his last few months on earth. But for the first time, Jenny thought that Aunt Georgie had truly fallen in love.

"Yes, darling, I was *very* fond of him. I still am. But the funeral was months ago and I'm old. I have to move on while I can. I took a cruise to get my mind off sad things."

"You are not that old, and you don't have to move on so quickly." Jenny's voice dropped, and she cleared her throat to recover it. Whatever haunted her aunt—taking cruises was not going to evict her ghosts.

"Oh, but I do. I do, darling. Once you're as old as I am, you'll see."

"Well, either way, though... You said you would visit and see us in Mendocino Cove."

It sounded too much like a demand. It was a tactical error.

"No, I don't think I will after all. I'm in the Bahamas, darling, and the first dinner bell just rang. I have some nice people on my table. The captain too."

Maybe those were gulls screaming in the background—or possibly children playing in a pool?

"Can we at least talk really quick?" Jenny said.

"Well...okay, if it is really quick. What do you want?"

It wasn't the most auspicious beginning, but Jenny had to try. "My daughter Audrey is a hotel manager," Jenny said, counting on the fact that her aunt had effectively wiped their last three conversations from her memory. "We would like to reopen the hotel for business. Of course, we would split the profit, and you would get a share."

"Oh, I don't know about the hotel. I'll have to think about it," Aunt Georgie said. She sounded uncomfortable.

Her aunt wanted to forget about the hotel. She certainly didn't need more money. But Jenny hastened on. "That's fine—let's talk again in a week, okay? Aunt Georgie, there's another thing... I found a letter from Grandma Rosie to me in the house. She wrote that she wanted to leave me a few family heirlooms. They're antiques and might be worth something. I haven't had anything appraised yet because I wanted to tell you about this first."

"You already got your mother's share of the inheritance," Aunt Georgie said. "There was no mention of any heirlooms in the will."

"No, there wasn't, I realize that. But Grandma hid a note for me. It sort of was a treasure hunt. I guess she thought it wasn't necessary to include a clause in the will?"

"Well, I don't know, darling. It's not that I don't want you to have money and things. But what if everything in that hotel is cursed?"

Jenny sighed. "I live here, Aunt Georgie, and I promise nothing is cursed. Would you consider letting me have the heirlooms, please? Grandma wanted me to have them. I can show you the note she wrote. And...right now I can really use money and things."

"You can?"

"Yes, very much. Some of the heirlooms I would like to keep for their sentimental value. But others I would like to sell. I need some money to get back on my feet."

"Are you sure nothing's haunted?"

"Of course nothing's haunted, Aunt Georgie. The hotel is lovely, full of love and light and warmth. Come back home and see for yourself."

Aunt Georgie ignored that. "Can I loop back to why you need money, darling?" There was a spark of interest in the words.

"Well, my husband died, remember? And he...well, he lost the business and the houses and also our savings and the retirement money."

"That's right... Steve. I never liked him in the first place."

"Stan. You did like him, Aunt Georgie."

"Well, darling, send me a photo of that note and... I don't know, maybe a list of the heirlooms Mom was talking about."

"Sure. I will do that. Thank you for considering it."

"Oh! That was the second bell. I really do have to go, Jenny, darling."

"Only...Aunt Georgie, if you let Audrey reopen the hotel, she will stay here with me. I would love nothing more than having her live in Mendocino Cove with me."

"Ah."

"Will you please think it over very carefully? The hotel is empty. We can give it another go."

"Darling, I *have* to go. Say hi to Aubrey for me, will you?"

"Her name is Audrey," Jenny said with a sinking heart. "Yes, I'll tell her. I'll call you in a week."

But Aunt Georgie had already hung up.

A light knock on the door interrupted Jenny's staring at the phone. "Come in, sweetheart."

Audrey opened the door. She leaned against the jamb and crossed her arms. "Your face looks like seven weekends of rain," she said. "Did you just talk to your aunt?"

"Yes," Jenny said and let her hand with the phone sink on her lap. "Sweetie, I think you had better look for another job in town, at least until she makes up her mind. Maybe now that Hannah is so busy with her food truck, Michael will consider hiring another waitress at the Mermaid Galley."

"I see," Audrey said quietly. "I guess I'll drive over and ask him." She pushed off the jamb and turned, but then she stopped and looked back over her shoulder. "It's so stupid, though," she said bitterly. "Here is this gorgeous old hotel, empty and falling to ruin, and I have my degree in running it."

Jenny stood, brushing her hair back.

Unlike her, Audrey had never met carefree, brave, sweet young Georgie. She hadn't watched how love and grief for her sister Willow had pulled Georgie into a hole so deep and with walls so steep she'd never managed to climb out again. In despair, Georgie had started to claw at the walls like a trapped animal, digging narrow tunnels of distraction and superstition that led nowhere.

"The hotel is neither empty nor falling to ruin, darling," Jenny said firmly. "We live here. At least Georgie lets us do that much. You should have heard her. I genuinely think she's scared of this place and that it won't do us good."

Audrey shrugged angrily. "Is she at least coming so we can show it to her?"

Compassion welled up in Jenny at the look in her daughter's eyes. Audrey loved this place. After her father's suicide and the loss of her old world, it was a connection to her family. It held beauty and consistency and the past, and Audrey wanted to strengthen that connection. She needed this place. She wanted to be part of a history, and she had to make some small contribution of her own.

Suddenly, Jenny felt an overwhelming fear that if Audrey couldn't find work and left Mendocino Cove now, in this state, she would end up like her great-aunt Georgie. Anchorless, drifting from here to there, never grounded and never at home.

Jenny went and grabbed Audrey before her daughter could stomp off, hugging her close. "She's not going to come," Jenny said firmly. "It doesn't matter. Forget Georgie; she's my problem. *We* live here, okay? I will make enough money for you to stay. I literally don't care what you do as long as you feel at home. Write cookbooks. Compose music. Film wedding dress unboxing videos. It doesn't matter. But stay long enough that Mendocino Cove feels like your home. Promise me that."

Audrey turned and wrapped her arms around Jenny, resting her head against her shoulder. "But that's the problem, Mom," she murmured. "It already feels too much like home."

A wave of relief washed through Jenny. "That's good."

"Is it? Is it good when it *feels* like home, but it isn't home?"

"Ah," Jenny murmured into her daughter's beach-scented hair.

The hotel belonged to Georgie, and there was not much Jenny could do to change that. Empty as the place was, Georgie would never sell. Aside from that little fact, real estate prices had soared sky-high since Jenny was paid out her share of the hotel. She'd never be able to buy the hotel back on an educator's salary. "Let's take baby steps. Maybe we should invite River again to come visit us."

Audrey nodded.

"And maybe we should go to the winery and see if Jon's around," Jenny continued. Despite Jenny's fears, Audrey had fully approved of her mother's relationship with her childhood sweetheart and even liked him. "We'll open a bottle of wine and sit on the terrace, okay?"

"Yes." Audrey swallowed and straightened back up again, squaring her shoulders. "But first, let's stop by the Mermaid Galley and see if Michael needs a new waitress."

CHAPTER 5

A gull screamed into Ava's ear. Her eyes flew open, and she was wide awake instantly. "Oh, my goodness." She laughed. "You scared me."

The gull wasn't in the room. Behind the sheer curtains blowing in the morning breeze, Ava could see the bird's silhouette. The gull squished itself into the flower box in front of the window and was sitting as best it could on a soft, cascading pillow of pink sweet alyssum. Every time it flapped a wing for balance, it screamed angrily.

"Find a better spot to sit, Miss Gull. One that actually fits you," Ava murmured. "Believe me, I was trying too long to fit into the wrong spot too. I know what I'm talking about."

As if it listened, the gull spread its wings and took off, disappearing into the nebulous morning. Already, the sun was burning holes through the dense mists that rolled in from the water. It was a sure sign that the day was going to be beautiful.

Her bed was too cozy and comfortable to get up, so Ava turned on her side and picked up her phone from the honey-colored nightstand. She had muted her notifications, but when she checked her messages, a text was waiting for her.

It was from Bruno. With a sigh, Ava opened the text.

I'm off to play a round of golf. Are you at your mother's?

Of course, he was off to play a round of golf. He wasn't doing much else. The golf course was his summer office.

Bruno was always busy. For a long time, Ava had been in denial about how lonely she was in her empty nest. She worked hard to justify the time he spent anywhere but at home because it made the lack of intimacy and connection more bearable.

Bruno was working for the family. He was working because he was creative and needed the outlet. He was well-respected and had many professional obligations. He was this, he was that. He was everything but there for Ava.

Before he was made partner, she'd often felt like a box to check on Bruno's to-do list.

Afterward, she felt like her checkbox didn't even make the list anymore.

At first, she'd gone by the textbook. She couldn't expect her husband to read her mind, so she was going to communicate her needs. Ava scheduled a date and time as if she were a client, prepared friendly I-statements, and reminded herself to listen and stay calm. Using careful phrases, she conveyed her need to see Bruno now and then. She was hoping they could talk with each other sometimes, have dinner together once in a blue moon, sleep in each other's arms again instead of turning their backs.

It didn't help. Bruno listened with a stony mask on his face, saying little. What he did say was that he had too much to do to deal with it right now. Soon, it would get better. The pressure would release, but not right now. It was probably missing Zoe that made Ava think it was his fault. Didn't she have friends? Maybe do a little more yoga and make new ones?

They didn't even finish the dinner. Ava had felt sick to the stomach.

The final turn of the screw came when Bruno retired.

She'd waited for him to retire the way a sailor's bride waits for her man's ship to return to port. But when it did, Bruno only stepped on land to play golf.

Every day, all day, he seemed to putter around the course while dictating letters or notes or emails to his secretary, Ginny. Ginny wore short white golfing skirts and tight polo shirts in blush pastels and knew everyone in their country club by name. More than once, Ava had arrived in search of her husband and found him sitting at a table with Ginny, talking and laughing as they recovered from their last round of whatever it was they'd been doing.

Ava first grew angry, and then she stopped talking. Bruno was smart. He understood what she had told him. He just didn't care.

The only thing left to do was for Ava to tell Bruno in so many words that she wanted a divorce.

It should be easy enough. Zoe led her own life. Ava had some money of her own. But she also had been with Bruno for all of her adult life and saying the word divorce would end an era.

It was going to be hard. She had come home to Mendocino Cove to root herself for the coming storm.

Visiting a friend back home, Ava texted Bruno and dropped the phone like a hot stone. She rolled on her back, closed her eyes, pulled her duvet up to her chin, and inhaled the salty air.

The bedsheets were made from Portuguese linen, Billie had told her, and had been washed so often they were as soft as feather down. They smelled of lavender too, and of...coffee?

Ava opened her eyes again.

The bright sun was drying up the mist and lit up Billie's pretty little guestroom. Whenever the sea breeze made the sheer curtains dance, the light found a new path. It shone on the honey pine furniture, the framed seascapes on the wall, the wood floor that generations of feet had scuffed into a cheerful gleam, and the door with the hook that held Ava's bathrobe.

"Oh, okay. Fine." She sat up and pushed the lavender-scented duvet back.

Billie's cottage was not the place to be in a bad mood.

Ava swung her feet on the ground, taking a second to make sure the floor felt as good as it looked, and then she went into the small bathroom, splashed her face with water, ran a wet brush through her hair, and put on sunscreen. Then she pulled back the curtains and opened the window.

The air smelled like perfume, of sea and salt and cypresses. Ava turned out her bed, and then she dug through her duffle bag.

She didn't need much. Fresh underwear and a pair of highwater jeans, a white blouse with short sleeves, and a summer cardigan for the morning. Once dressed, Ava stepped into a pair of well-worn navy leather flats and made her way downstairs.

She found her host in the sun-flooded kitchen. A double-wide door opened to a small garden full of fragrant mint and lemon balm, and birds were singing outside. Ava knocked on the wooden doorjamb to announce herself. "Good morning."

"Good morning!" Billie looked up from kneading dough on the flour-dusted kitchen island. "I thought you'd sleep longer." She wiped her hands, then turned off the audiobook playing from a small speaker. "Did I clang my pots too loud?" She smiled.

"I only heard the gull that's nesting in your alyssum." Ava smiled back. "What are you making?"

"It's bread dough for tomorrow." Billie stopped kneading and cut the ball of dough with a sharp knife. "Good enough," she said, studying the happy little bubbles in the dough. "Ava, help yourself to coffee. It's piping hot."

While Ava filled a mug with steaming coffee that smelled of freshly roasted beans, Billie scooped the dough into a blue enamel bowl and covered it with a clean tea towel. "I'll punch it down one more time later," she announced. "Maybe after I call my health insurance and ask about that weird charge on my doctor's bill last week."

"You went to the doctor?"

Billie carried the bowl to a warm spot. "I needed help to get a splinter out of my foot, and I wasn't about to ask a friend for help on that one."

Ava chuckled. "I'll take you out for a mani-pedi if you like."

Billie laughed. "I'll take you up on it. It won't do much good for my beachy feet, but it won't hurt either. Are you hungry?"

"A little," Ava admitted, feeling guilty.

Billie nodded, looking satisfied. "I set the breakfast table on the dock. I like my ground to sway a little while I eat my chocolate croissant. How about you?"

"I don't have a firm opinion when it comes to swaying grounds," Ava said. "But I'm open-minded."

"There you go, that's where it's at." Billie untied her apron, opened the oven, and pulled out a breadbasket that had been waiting inside. "Grab your coffee and the carafe, and follow me."

CHAPTER 6

Carrying the coffee, Ava followed her old friend through the garden and across the lawn. They stepped on the wide dock, and only then did the breakfast table materialize. The sun had burned off most of the morning mist near the cottage, but down here, it still veiled the Pacific Ocean that lapped at the dock.

Billie set the breadbasket on the already laden breakfast table and sat.

Surprised, Ava put down her carafe and sat down across from Billie. "Goodness, have you made all this yourself? I hope you didn't put yourself out for me. I usually just have oatmeal with blueberries."

"Jon made half of it," Billie said. "He gets up early too, and we always make enough for breakfast to swap. Okay, let's see. On the plate to your right are croque madame sandwiches with ham and cheese."

Ham and cheese sandwich didn't do justice to the crusty bread that was layered with Italian ham, Gruyère, and béchamel sauce, toasted golden and topped with a poached egg.

"In the breadbasket are croissants," Billie continued. "The square ones have chocolate in them."

"Chocolate," Ava repeated obediently. She swallowed.

"Jon brought over the crêpes Suzettes. I have to give it to him. They're fantastic."

"Can I take one?" Despite her cake feast the day before, Ava's stomach was suddenly so empty it growled.

"Absolutely," Billie said. "Go ahead."

"Someone help me." Ava lifted one of the thin, delicate pancakes onto her plate and tried it. It was still warm and slathered in a luscious sauce made from caramelized sugar, butter, orange juice, and orange zest.

"He makes them with a splash of orange liquor," Billie declared and took a croissant from the basket. She broke it open, exposing the flaky, buttery interior, and sighed happily. "This is my favorite way to start the day. Good food, good company, and a beautiful view." She spread bright-red raspberry jam on her croissant.

Ava had finished her crepe already. "It takes like heaven," she said.

"I'll let him know." Billie bit into her breakfast. "Try the food I made."

Ava ate a whole croque madame, and then, even though she was definitely full, she simply had to try one of Billie's chocolate croissants. It was so flaky and soft and chewy; Ava almost swooned and had one more. She felt terribly greedy and guilty. But everything tasted so good. So, so good.

Ava had eaten oatmeal with blueberries religiously every morning for the last two or three years. She'd never felt like she was missing out. Until now. Maybe a treat now and then would not damage her health or her waistline so very much.

Billie chatted about her animals, telling stories about sea lions and pelicans. Ava listened while she savored the exquisite tastes and admired the fog-covered ocean.

Billie's job was fulfilling and clearly made her happy.

Ava smiled. Not for the first time, she wished she had kept writing.

She had loved researching and putting together articles and features for women's magazines. She loved meeting with cowriters and editors, participating in panel discussions and the eventual writing workshop.

But once her little family had claimed her time, Ava's writing income fizzled to a drop on a hot stone compared to Bruno's salary. Ava's contacts fell out of touch and one by one either retired or simply disappeared.

"Have the last pancake," Billie said suddenly. "They don't reheat well."

"I wish I could, but I stuffed my face enough. I'm sorry about eating so much," Ava apologized and set her fork and knife on the plate. Her waistband already felt tighter than yesterday.

Billie glanced at her. "Don't worry about it for a second," she said after a moment. "I love it when people eat. I like feeding them. Baking and cooking for the day is my morning meditation. I tried yoga, but it didn't take. Baking raisin buns and poaching eggs did. I'd much rather my friends eat it than have to throw it away. And I'd just like to mention that you didn't eat all that much. Faye is a head shorter than you, and she easily eats twice your breakfast."

"Well, I'm so glad." Ava exhaled a breath of relief. "Because Billie, this is the best food I've eaten in a long while, and I won't be able to resist whatever you make next, either. Your cooking gets all the stars I have to give."

"Thank you very much." Billie dunked a raisin bun into her coffee. "Look, the fog is lifting."

"It's so pretty." Ava was admiring the way the glittering water appeared where the mist receded when her phone buzzed.

"Sorry," she mumbled and glanced at the phone. Bruno again—he never texted, so why did he have to keep interrupting her now?

"I'll be back in a sec." Billie laid her linen napkin on the table and stood, grabbing the coffee carafe and taking it with her to the house.

Ginny is just my secretary, nothing more. You know that. Golfing helps me focus.

"Focus on what?" Ava murmured and tucked the phone away again. Bruno didn't ask a question; his text didn't require a response.

After a moment, she pulled her phone out again.

I'm no longer competing with Ginny or golf for your attention. I'm also not interested in hearing about them.

Her thumb hesitated for a moment, but then she sent the text.

"You okay?" Billie sat back down and poured them both fresh coffee.

"Yes," Ava said and put the phone on silent before she slipped it in her pocket. "It's my marriage. I'm over it."

"Tell me all the dirty details." Billie sank back in her chair.

"It's the same old story." Ava shook her head. "Boy meets girl, boy loses girl, boy finds girl... It only ends there for the lucky ones, doesn't it? It's not my ending, anyway. In my marriage it went on with boy retreats from girl, girl fights to be close, boy retreats further, girl figures out much too late that she is wasting time."

"I do think I've heard that story before," Billie said. "And for me, throw in boy cheats on girl. I got divorced when the boys were still little."

"I'm not sure I wouldn't prefer a harsh end to the slow, lonely death my marriage went through."

"Oh, Ava." Billie frowned in commiseration. "Is it that bad?"

Ava nodded. "I held on until he retired. I thought it would be a new start and everything would be better. But he only swapped the office for the golf course and now works while also golfing."

"Did you talk to him about it?"

"I tried, but now I just have to face the fact that he doesn't love me. He hasn't loved me in...goodness. Decades? Maybe never. Though in the beginning it felt real enough." She swallowed.

"You seem very collected," Billie remarked after a while. "Doesn't it hurt?"

"I think I already went through most of my stages of grief," Ava said after a moment. "There's that song... I don't know the words off the top of my head, but she sings about how she can buy herself flowers and how she loves herself better than he can. It made me cry when I first heard it. And then I recognized that yes—I *can* love myself better than Bruno. So I bought myself flowers at my favorite florist's, went home, and called you about a visit home."

"Sounds like you have made up your mind," Billie said. "Does it feel good to have made the decision? I was relieved when I finally did."

Ava picked at the crumbs on her plate. "No, it doesn't feel good to me. It feels like pulling on big girl panties. It feels like cold, hard truth and stark reality. I don't like feeling like that. I want fairy-tale endings and eyes full of love and a tender hand in the small of my back."

"I know," Billie said. "Reality has a way of forcing its way into our fairy tales, doesn't it?"

"I couldn't stay in it any longer," Ava agreed sadly. "My last hope went the way of Bruno's golf balls—into a hole in the ground. My brain no longer lets my heart pretend I'm loved."

"Do you still love him?" Billie asked.

Ava shrugged. The question made her uncomfortable. "It doesn't matter if I do," she said. "I can't love both myself and Bruno at the same time anymore. One love has to go for the other to be possible, and I finally decided to love myself. I only have a few years left, and I want to make the most out of them. If I have to buy my own flowers, at least I don't want to be angry that he doesn't do it."

"You have plenty of years left. But you made the right call when you decided to take care of yourself first," Billie said and handed Ava the last chocolate croissant.

It was still a bit warm in her hand. Ava sighed. "I know why I'm eating everything and their uncle, Billie," she said. "It's for comfort. It's to stuff the gaping hole in my heart."

Billie smiled in understanding. "And so what? If your soul wants comfort, give it comfort. Eat freshly baked croissants and drink coffee with cream and sugar. Sleep in, go swimming with friends, and drink wine at beach bonfires. This is not the time to watch your waist and mind that you cross your ankles. Go fall in love with another man. Have a fling. If you do decide to love yourself, you might as well do it properly!"

Ava bit into the sweet croissant without taking her eyes off Billie. "Food and friends and bonfires, yes," she said with a full mouth. "Men, no. No thank you. I don't need that sort of aggravation ever again."

"Well, there aren't any eligible men left in Mendocino Cove anyway, last time I looked," Billie said loyally. "By the way, what is it you would like to do today?"

"I want to visit our old haunts," Ava said. Talking about facing reality had settled on her mood like fog on water. "I'd love to drive by my old place. I always wondered what became of it after that Silicon Valley millionaire bought it from my parents."

"Your old house?" Billie didn't look too sure. "Honestly—I don't recommend stopping by."

"What?" Ava looked up. "Why not?"

CHAPTER 7

"What are you doing, Ava? We're almost at your old house, and you haven't opened your eyes for the last mile. Are you awake, or did breakfast put you into a food coma?" Billie flicked the blinker and turned her pickup truck into the street. "Just checking in because we're in your old street. Last chance to change your mind and come to Jon's instead of seeing your old house."

At Billie's first words, Ava had opened her eyes. She smiled and stretched, feeling as if she had just woken up from sleeping, not daydreaming—warm and comfortable and cozy, despite Billie's misgivings over her visit to her childhood home. "I haven't changed my mind."

Billie rolled down the driver's window and rested her arm on it, and the warm slipstream played with her short curls. "Then why close your eyes?"

"I wanted to remember the house one more time the way it used to be. It was such a pretty house." Ava's parents had loved their home, and it had shown.

Billie glanced over. "It doesn't look like that anymore."

"I'm just glad they didn't tear it down." Ava closed her eyes again. "I'm walking through the house in my mind," she said. "I'm almost done."

Again, she pictured the pretty and picturesque arts and crafts house. Nestled amidst oak trees and cypresses at the very end of a long street, it had plenty of whimsical charm and even more unique architectural details that added warmth and interest to both the outside and the inside. A knock on the door by a curious stranger was quite normal. The house was often featured in regional architectural magazines, and Mom or Dad would happily take their visitors on a tour, showing them around and offering a cup of tea in the garden.

The house was photographed for magazines because of the stunning backdrop of the Pacific Ocean. The sparkling blue contrasted beautifully with the exterior, which was a blend of warm earth tones with a combination of stone, brick, and timber elements that added character. The front porch was adorned with hand-crafted wooden pillars and flower boxes that overflowed with petunias, forget-me-nots, and geraniums. It was the perfect spot to enjoy a cup of tea in the shade or wave at neighbors passing by.

Large, multi-paned windows with stained glass cast colorful patterns on the hardwood floors inside. Exposed wooden beams spanned the open ceilings, and a twisting, freestanding staircase led to the second floor.

The living room sported a charming fireplace framed by an intricately carved mantelpiece that looked like something out of a hobbit hole. The room had been the family's main hangout spot, filling Ava with a feeling of comfort and tranquility. Mom had collected vintage furniture and Dad eclectic artwork; both effortlessly blended the past and the present in the house.

A sunlit studio, tucked away behind a hidden door, overlooked the lush garden from large windows. Its walls were hung with Dad's colorful paintings in progress, and wooden shelves were lined with jars filled with brushes, tubes and pots of oil and acrylics, and a thousand other things. Ava remembered their heady and distinctive smells well enough. She'd loved spending time there, either playfully mixing her own colors on the little palette he'd gifted her or watching her father create his art.

The kitchen had a rustic farmhouse sink, pretty bands of Moroccan mosaic tiles, and open shelving that held Mom's eclectic mix of vintage china and hand-thrown pottery. Mom used to twirl all day in and out of the kitchen, singing songs about selkies and the fair folk in her high, clear soprano while she baked huckleberry pies and cooked the family's meals in between making her own art. A door opened from the kitchen into the spacious winter garden that was made of glass and welded metal and housed Mom's pottery wheel and blocks of clay, furnace, glazes, and living edge shelves full of teapots and plates for sale.

Ava sighed. Oh, and the backyard... It used to have a flower garden bursting with blooms, a small koi pond, winding stone pathways, and a cozy nook beneath a sprawling oak tree that was perfect for reading adventure novels. There were fruit trees too—crooked old apples, pears, and cherries—and a small kitchen bed dotted with ripe tomatoes and fragrant herbs. The garden was on a bluff, with the blue sea sparkling below. It was once a happy home. A place where kids played, laughter echoed throughout the halls, and love filled every corner.

"Okay. Almost there. Hope you're ready," Billie said, and the rhythmic rumbling of her pickup's engine slowed.

Ava opened her eyes and blinked. They were in her old street, passing the last neighbor. Her house was tucked out of sight at the end of the street.

And there it was, her house.

Ava couldn't suppress a small sound of dismay.

More exactly, there was the broken shell of her house.

"I told you it wasn't good." Billie pulled up in front of the house. "Though it's much worse than it was last time I checked."

"What *happened*?" Ava couldn't believe her eyes. "Who would let a house like that just fall to ruin?"

Billie shook her head. "I don't understand it, either. Some random shack, maybe. But a gorgeous arts and crafts house? The new owner must have simply forgotten the house."

Ava leaned over to peer through the window. "I want to check it out. You go see your brother like you meant to, Billie. You don't have to wait for me."

"What are you going to do?" Billie asked, sounding suspicious.

"Nothing, of course. I just want to look around."

"Okay, I'll pick you up on my way back. But be careful," Billie warned. "You're trespassing. Don't go inside if you find a way in. The roof and floors might be rotten. Who knows if it's structurally sound?"

"I promise to watch out. Thanks so much for dropping me off. See you later, Billie." Ava got out of the pickup truck and closed the door. With a wave, Billie turned and drove off, and Ava went to the garden gate.

Moss and lichens grew on the steps and on the tiled roof. Vines crawled up the wood detail, and weeds and wildflowers had taken over the once carefully tended front yard. Ava pushed them aside with her foot as she picked her way through flowers and ferns. It was better not to think about all the loving care—not to mention hard work—her parents had put into cultivating the garden.

One of the columns of the front porch had cracked, and the porch roof, no longer properly supported, was lopsided. Ava gingerly stepped onto the porch. The dry wood creaked, but nothing wiggled or wobbled or threatened to fall on her head, so she proceeded to the front door. It still had the brass knocker that was shaped like a seahorse.

She tried to lift it, but it wouldn't move. Brass didn't rust, so maybe the cute, custom-made knocker was still salvageable?

The street was empty. Even back then, only neighbors and people specifically searching for the house would come this far down the dead-end street. Billie's warning not to go inside echoed around Ava's head, but surely, if she was careful...

She stepped off the porch again. Dad used to hide the key under it, and she knew he had forgotten to take it when they moved because they'd been laughing about it in Seattle.

Ava squatted and pushed away the weeds beside the stairs, shining her phone flashlight through the broken lattice woodwork. Already, her heart was beating harder. She usually did her best to follow rules; now, she was trespassing even by being on the property.

What would happen if she was caught going inside?

She hesitated. But what would happen if she didn't? How many more opportunities would she get at a last glimpse?

All her life she'd been a law-abiding citizen, a good mother, a faithful wife.

She should stop and leave it be, enjoy the beautiful walk back to Billie's cottage instead of breaking and entering. On the other hand, this one transgression would hurt nobody but possibly herself.

Obviously, the owner didn't care about the house. It wasn't like she was going to steal anything or sue him if a board fell on her head.

If the key worked, she would lock the door again once she was done.

It would be like nothing ever happened. The dull glow lit up weeds and dead leaves. Ava peered through the lattice, stopping when the light glinted off a small glass jar perched on the sloping stone ledge.

Feeling like a thief, Ava maneuvered a hand carefully through the broken latticework to reach it, scared that some kind of animal might appear from beneath the foliage at any moment. With trembling fingers, she inched the jar out from its hiding spot and inspected its contents. The key was still there, still intact after all this time.

The metal lid was stuck tightly. Ava exhaled and shook out her aching head.

Then, before she could chicken out, Ava took the small jar to a nearby rock and shattered it into pieces before quickly tying them in a tissue and stuffing them in her bag. The key remained unscathed. She stood, holding the relic in her hand before returning to the front door and slipping it into the lock. To her amazement, it fit perfectly. Hesitantly, she twisted it until she heard a click and saw the door creak open just enough for her to slip inside.

"Hello?" she called out, her voice wavering with nerves. "Anyone here? Can I come in?"

Nobody protested. Only a wasp zoomed over her head to freedom.

Ava couldn't help but feel a pang of sadness when she pushed the door wider, and the hinges creaked in protest. This door used to open all day long for friends and neighbors.

"Oh boy, Ava," she admonished herself in a whisper as she entered. "You're officially crossing the line now."

Heeding Billie's warning about safety, Ava tiptoed gingerly through the entrance hall. A confusing mix of memory and reality, of childhood and adulthood, of grief and anger swept through her as she passed the fireplace. The multi-paned windows still cast colorful patterns, but the once gleaming hardwood floors were dusty and scuffed. The exposed wooden beams still crossed the ceiling, but spiderwebs stretched along them.

Ava put a foot on the first step of the freestanding staircase. It gave her a nervous feeling, but nothing moved or groaned in protest. She carefully climbed step by step, ready to retreat at the first suspicious sound, and soon, she was on the second floor.

Each room had its own character. She paused in the door of her own old bedroom. The walls were still adorned with Dad's hand-painted murals of mermaids and sea creatures. Of course, there was no longer any furniture—but Ava could still see the lighter spots on the wall where her horse posters had hung.

"Weird," she whispered to relieve the unnatural silence and moved on.

The bathroom looked rough. In one place, the ceiling had caved in. Ava peered into the hole to the attic. What had caused the damage? Had a storm knocked a large branch of one of the old oaks?

The large bathtub was dirty and rusted, and the stained glass in front of the window was broken. Colorful shards lay like sprinkles on the patterned floor tiles. The walls that used to be a soft blue, reminiscent of the ocean, had large dark patches.

"Water damage," she whispered to herself. Maybe a pipe had burst, and the ceiling board had rotted through. It didn't smell of mold, luckily. Hopefully, the damage was fixable.

Ava turned away with a frown. Who bought a house just to let it rot?

The wood of the next bedroom door she tried had warped, locking into place. Ava didn't want to rattle it too hard and made her way back down without looking into the other bedrooms.

Back in the living room, she tried the sliding door to the garden. It worked, though it needed oil. Ava stepped outside.

Despite the overgrown weeds, crumbling stones, and the dried-out koi pond, the garden was still stunningly beautiful. Vines of wildflowers had sprouted up, and the air was thick with the scent of jasmine and lavender. The sea breeze carried the sound of waves crashing against the bluff, and for a moment, Ava closed her eyes and let herself be transported back to a time when this was a happy home.

When she opened her eyes, a sudden idea struck her. Why couldn't this house be a happy home again? Her happy home? Who said she had to go back to Seattle?

Nobody really.

With some elbow grease, money, and plenty of love, the house could be restored to its former glory. She could picture it—the garden cleaned up, pruned and blooming, the woodwork fixed. She could even bring Mom's furniture and Dad's paintings back from Seattle.

Bruno wasn't likely to miss them.

Ava knew it wouldn't be an easy task, but as she stood there, surrounded by the beauty of the garden and the memories of the past, she knew it was worth it. This house by the sea deserved to be loved and appreciated once again.

As she walked back through the house, her cheeks warmed with new plans for the future. Her footsteps quickened with anticipation, and by the time she had once again locked the doors and slipped the key back into her pocket, she was smiling.

CHAPTER 8

The evening sun dipped the vineyard into molten gold, pouring off the sky and onto the long rows of vines that trailed over rolling hills. The juicy clusters of grapes gleamed like backlit sea glass, while the old oaks and cypresses shone brightly like pictures from a fairy-tale book.

Faye and her friends had snagged one of the long picnic tables on the roofed terrace. It was especially pleasant outside; both temperature and humidity couldn't be more pleasant if they tried, and the hum of voices and laughter was quieter than inside the pretty tasting room.

Faye shielded her eyes against the sinking sun. She was positively, absolutely, starving. Hannah and Nick, the teenager Jon had hired to help out, were bringing the food.

"Grilled salmon with citrus glaze?" Hannah called out. Billie and Gabe, Faye's date, lifted their hands. Dutifully, their plates of grilled filet of salmon, drizzled with a tangy citrus glaze and served alongside a medley of roasted vegetables and a bed of fluffy quinoa, danced through several pairs of hands until they reached their destination.

"Who ordered the braised short ribs with red wine reduction?"

Faye looked up at her friend. "Me. Thank you, Hannah."

Hannah smiled. "You do look peckish, Faye, all pale and big-eyed. I'm glad you got the ribs. Here you go." She put down a huge plate of tender, succulent short ribs. "They are slow-cooked in a rich red wine reduction, and I gave you extra creamy mashed potatoes and sautéed seasonal greens," she said cheerfully.

Faye took a deep breath. "Thanks. It looks delicious." She exhaled.

"Uh. What's this here again?" Nick nervously asked Hannah and held up a plate he was holding.

She raised an eyebrow at the question. Hannah took her food very seriously. "Roasted beet and goat cheese salad."

"That's mine." Jenny held out her hands, and Nick handed her the vibrant salad with roasted beets, creamy goat cheese, candied walnuts, and fresh arugula, drizzled with a balsamic vinaigrette.

Nick slid the last two plates heaped high with creamy and velvety mushroom risotto in front of Audrey and Jon.

"Oh, smell this," Audrey called out and held up her plate so Faye, who sat opposite her, could take a whiff. "Smell the truffle oil! I *love* truffles."

With that one aromatic whiff, Faye's appetite left. "Goodness... yes, that's very fragrant. Nice." Faye held her breath until Audrey pulled the plate away.

Everyone started digging in; they'd come here so Jon, who owned the vineyard, could eat with them. And eating was what they were going to do.

Faye dipped a fork into her red wine reduction and put it down again.

Gabe leaned over to her. "Would you rather have the salmon? Or a salad?" he asked quietly.

She tried to smile. "No, thank you. I think I'm getting a migraine."

"A migraine?" He put down his fork and knife without as much as a regretful glance at his sumptuous dinner. "Would you like to go home?"

"You've been working all day. You should eat. Maybe it will go away." Going home was exactly what Faye wanted, but she could hold out until her man had eaten. Gabe was a detective, and the call of duty came often enough without any regard for his meal or bedtimes.

"I'll be quick." He squeezed her hand and started eating.

Faye reached for a leaf of Audrey's salad and bit into it. No way was she able to eat meat. And the sun was suddenly too bright. A wave of nausea overcame her, and she put the salad leaf on her plate, trying not to breathe in the scents of her food. "I'm going to... Excuse me for a second." She stood.

Gabe stopped eating and threw her a sharp-eyed glance. "Should I be worried?"

"No. No. It's fine. I just need a moment to...you know." She did her best to look reassuringly. His frown told her that it didn't work.

"I'll come with you. I'd like to wash my hands before I eat," Jenny said quietly and stood. "Come on, Faye."

Together, they walked to the bathroom. Jenny washed her hands while Faye slipped into one of the stalls, grateful for the cleanliness and the crisp lemon scent.

She couldn't decide whether she wanted to cry or throw up, and so she stood, miserable and bent slightly at the hip, eyes closed. Because if she was going to look at the toilet and there was even a speck out of order...

The rushing of water in Jenny's sink stopped. "Hey. What's going on, Faye? Want me to drive you home?"

Beads formed on Faye's temples. "You don't want me in your car right now," she pressed through clenched teeth.

"I can always tie you to the roof rack," Jenny said. "Do you have an upset stomach? Did you eat anything iffy?"

Just as sudden as it had come, the nausea left. Faye took a huge gulp of air, relieved that it was over. She unlocked the door and teetered out.

"Sheesh, girl. You're green. Sit here." Jenny took Faye's hand and led her to the chair.

Faye sat, and Jenny handed her a wad of moist paper towels. "Put that on your neck."

Faye blotted her temples and forehead and then pressed the cool towels on her neck as instructed. She laughed weakly. "It comes and goes," she said. "This was definitely the worst wave yet. Thanks for sticking with me, Jen."

"What do you think it is? Food poisoning? What did you eat today?"

"It's not food poisoning." Faye exhaled sharply. "Let's not mention food for a sec."

"Fever?" Jenny reached out to touch her forehead.

Usually, Faye loved the scent of the winery's hand soap. Sometimes she went to wash her hands just for the fragrance of almonds and peaches. But now she recoiled from it.

Jenny dropped her hand and frowned. "What?"

"Sorry," Faye mumbled. "It's the smell of the soap. I can't stand it."

"Faye..." Jenny squatted in front of her. "Tell me this second what's going on, or I will call Gabe, an ambulance, and the police. I will also confiscate your phone. Maybe you're being blackmailed, and the stress is getting to you, but you can't talk about it."

"I'm sick to the stomach, not being blackmailed," Faye said. "It's just a summer cold gone awry."

"If you're sick to the stomach, why won't you go home? What are we doing here?"

Faye sighed, and with her breath, the last of the sickness disappeared.

Suddenly, she felt entirely normal again. "If I leave every time I feel sick, I would have been home all week. It's weird." She propped her elbows on her knees and buried her face in her hands. "Either it's a summer cold, or I'm pregnant."

Jenny stood. "Okay, so...it's not a cold, sweetie, and it's not morning sickness at six o'clock in the evening, either. I think you need to see a doctor."

Faye dropped her hands. "Did you have morning sickness when you were pregnant?"

"Luckily not. I was spared that entire ordeal."

Faye pulled off the warm wad of paper towels and tossed it. "Because the internet says you can get sick at any time of the day. It's not only in the morning."

Slowly, Jenny's hand went to her mouth. "Are you serious, Faye? Do you seriously think...?"

Faye straightened her back. "I don't know! I don't know, Jenny."

"You and Gabe..." Jenny tilted her head. "I mean, is it possible?"

"We weren't always as careful as we should have been," Faye admitted. "I mean, I'm forty-three. For the last ten years, all I seem to hear from doctors is perimenopause. Bad back? Perimenopause. Rash? Perimenopause. Fever and tummy ache? Same."

"I see." Jenny leaned against the sink. "Yeah, Faye... The peri part? That one can be tricky."

"I know." Faye took a couple of quick breaths. "I guess I sort of thought between the peri *and* being mostly careful... Plus, I haven't even done a test yet. It's probably an ulcer. Right?"

"Right." Jenny looked, sounded, and felt unconvinced. Faye could sense her vibration swinging in the frequency of, *well, sister, buckle yourself in because I got a whole hairy ball of news for you.*

"Maybe I should do a test?" Faye asked weakly.

"A test might not be the worst idea you've ever had," Jenny said gently.

"My worst one might've been when Gabe and I...uh. Never mind."

"Yeah, never mind." Jenny's smile had way too much pity in it. "What about Gabe?"

"What do you mean, what about Gabe?"

"Honey, you two have only just started to date. Does he know about"—Jenny vaguely circled her hand at Faye—"this entire situation?"

Faye buried her face again. She *couldn't* be pregnant. Could not. Not at forty-three, with a man she'd known for all of one month.

She took a bracing breath, slapped her knees with her hands, and stood. "I need to go buy a test."

Jenny nodded. "They sell them at the drugstore, honey pie."

Faye turned to go back to the others when something occurred to her. Very little escaped her sharp-eyed Sherlock. "Jenny?"

"What?"

"Will you buy a test for me and bring it over tomorrow morning right after Gabe leaves?" She opened the door.

Jenny followed her. "Yes, I will, you little coward," she whispered in Faye's ear as they walked back through the crowd to rejoin their friends.

CHAPTER 9

Lex?" Billie leaned forward and tapped her cousin's arm. For once, it was cloudy outside, and they were all inside enjoying the cozy afternoon and hoping for a night of rare and sorely needed rain.

Lex looked like a children's book illustration of a park ranger turned lumberjack with his broad shoulders and red flannel shirt. He lay on her sofa, crooked because he was too tall to fit, arms crossed, and frowning intently at the game replay on TV.

What game it was, Billie had no idea. Unlike their older cousins, she and Jon hadn't grown up watching sports. She was still supremely uninterested but tried not to let it show.

"Hey. Lex."

Lex looked up. "What's up, Billie?"

She smiled fondly at him. Her family had always been big and tight and local, and she enjoyed having Lex back in Mendocino Cove. After his dad's passing, Lex and his brother Brock had inherited the family lumber yard. Back home, Lex had finally worked through his hopes for a second chance with his former flame, Faye.

"Listen," Billie said. "We went to see Ava's house today."

Ava, who was reading a book on her phone in the armchair across from Billie, looked up.

"Ah," Lex said and smiled at Ava. "That can't have been easy."

Ava closed her book. "It wasn't. I don't get why anyone would let the house fall into ruin."

"Let me know if you need any lumber to fix it up." He grinned.

"I will," Ava said. "If I can get the owner to sell it back to me."

"Lex, sit up and focus," Billie said politely. "Do you know who owns the house? I sort of remember that it was a tech millionaire from Silicon Valley."

He didn't sit up. "Franklin? Was that the name? Dad was taking note of the deal back then."

Lex's dad, Harry, had been the unproclaimed king of Mendocino Cove. Nothing slipped by him unnoticed, least of all the sale of a local architectural gem to a stranger—tech millionaire or not.

"Yes, Franklin. I remember that name." Ava put her book on the coffee table. "Goodness, I wonder where the paperwork for the sale has gotten to. Dad wouldn't have thrown it away..." She hesitated. "Well, maybe he would have. I don't remember finding anything about it when I cleaned out his apartment after he passed."

Lex muted the game and swung his legs off the couch. "Are you really interested in buying it back, Ava?"

"I am," she declared and looked to Billie for support.

Billie nodded encouragement back. "It'd be much better for the town if Ava owned it," she said to her cousin. "But either way, it cannot be allowed to just rot. The ceiling caved in over the bathroom."

"The ceiling caved in?" Lex frowned. "I haven't been over there in I don't know how many years."

"It's so out of the way," Ava said. "It's not like people casually pass by. You really have to go looking for it."

"Hmm." Lex shook his head. "I mean, there are rules and regulations about that sort of thing, especially for buildings so close to the coast. Let me call an old friend real quick."

Billie looked at Ava, who smiled back. Lex always seemed to have an old friend who knew what to do.

Lex tapped on his phone. "Tom? This is Lex Donovan. How are you? Yes—hey, are you still up on the Coastal City Code?" He gave a thumbs-up as his friend answered, and then he put the call on speaker.

"We have a coastal house here in Mendocino Cove that is in pretty poor shape. The former owner is a friend and wants to know if there's a way to buy it back so she can fix it."

"Can you give me more details about the condition of the house?" Tom's hollow speaker voice asked.

Ava mouthed the information, and Lex repeated after her. "Just from driving by, it looks like roof damage, broken windows, and overgrown vegetation all around. It must've been like this for months, and it's becoming a safety hazard. My friend is worried someone might get hurt. She can send you pictures."

"Yes, send them over, and the address too. I'll come out for an inspection as soon as possible," Tom said. "Anything else I should know?"

"I don't have all the details, but I believe the owner's name is Franklin. My friend says it looks as if he's not been there in years."

"I'll track him down." Tom cleared his throat. "In the meantime, tell your friend to stay away. It doesn't sound safe, and it would also constitute trespassing."

Lex made a face at Ava, and she had the decency to look embarrassed. Billie grinned.

"Got it. Thanks, Tom. I owe you one."

"No worries, Lex. Send me the address now, okay? I'll make a couple of calls before I leave. Beats looking at my colleague's vacation photos."

I heard that, somebody called out in the background, and Tom laughed.

Lex chuckled. "If it comes up with the owner—let them know my friend is interested in buying the house back. Give them this phone number."

"I'll see what I can do. Send me photos and address."

Lex did as soon as Tom ended the call.

Not even an hour later, his phone rang. Lex switched off the TV and gestured to Ava that this was what they'd been waiting for.

Billie set a tray of crispy tortilla chips, lovingly piled high and generously adorned with a medley of toppings, on the sofa table. If Lex was working on her friend's behalf, the least Billie could do was feed him.

She plopped in her chair and took one of the loaded chips. The melted cheddar and Monterey Jack cheese created a creamy backdrop for generous dollops of tangy salsa, zesty guacamole, and cool sour cream. Billie carefully placed a slice of jalapeño for a touch of heat on top of another appetizing chip.

Ava put down her own phone. "Put it on speaker," she whispered.

Lex answered the call. "Hello?"

"Hi, this is Mr. Franklin's real estate manager, Timothy Meinhard. I was informed by the authorities that you reported the condition of Mr. Franklin's house in—uh, Mendocino Cove?"

"Yes, that's correct," Lex said. "Have you seen it lately? We're concerned about its state. It's falling down. We don't want a kid to go playing in it and have an accident happen."

"Mr. Franklin appreciates your concern. I must admit that I've been neglecting the property for far too long."

"I'm glad to hear that, Mr. Franklin. It's a nice little neighborhood. We'd like to keep it that way. Besides, that close to the coast, you have to be careful." He winked at Ava and crossed his fingers.

Billie popped another loaded chip into her mouth. This was more exciting than the game on TV.

"Actually, Mr. Franklin is considering selling the property," the agent said. "If you're interested, I'd be willing to offer it to you before listing it on the market—provided you take care of any fees incurred by code violations. Honestly, I have no idea whether there are any. It could be nothing, or it could be in the thousands. That'd be a risk you're taking."

Billie wiped her salty fingers on a napkin. It sounded very much as if Mr. Franklin had forgotten he owned the house. Had he ever known, or was it just part of a portfolio he purchased for tax or investment purposes?

Lex cleared his throat. "My friend is interested. I'll give you her number, or you can talk with her right now."

"Let me talk to her. Mr. Franklin is interested in a speedy and convenient solution."

Billie nodded at Ava—the agent couldn't wait to take the house off his list.

Ava took a deep breath. Her cheeks were flushed. "Hi," she said. "I'm Ava Allen. I'm interested in buying the house."

"Allen?" The agent rustled papers over on his end.

Billie tilted her head. Allen was Ava's maiden name, not her married name of Marshall.

"Yes, Mr. Franklin bought the house from my parents. I grew up there, and it holds a lot of special memories."

"Well, that sounds promising. I'm glad you contacted us, even if it was done through the authorities."

Ava inhaled. "I don't need to see the house before making an offer, but I would like to know what the asking price is."

Lex pushed a portion of nacho chips on his plate, and Billie had one more for good measure.

The agent explained that Mr. Franklin was open to any reasonable offers and that he wanted this transaction to go through as quickly as possible. Ava, who had spent the time between Lex's calls to research comps, offered what Billie thought was a fair sum for the property. It took into consideration potential code violations, as well as the fact that the building was basically abandoned. The agent seemed pleased with her bid and tentatively accepted the offer after some light negotiation.

"Can you believe it?" Ava looked giddy with excitement when she returned the phone to Lex.

Billie stood. "Baby, where is all that money going to come from?"

"I have the money." Ava ran her hands through her hair. "I have my parents' inheritance. I don't need my husband's permission to spend that, luckily."

"Yeah?"

"Yeah. Don't worry about that, Billie. It's not an issue. The price was less than Bruno paid for his summer golfing retreats over the last few years." Ava closed her eyes for a moment. "It's going to work out. I have my old house back."

"Ladies, I'm leaving." Lex checked his phone. "My dear brother needs me for the business."

They thanked Lex for his help and saw him off.

"Time for champagne!" Billie announced and went into the kitchen to get flutes and the bottle for pop-up celebrations.

When she came back out, Ava was lying on the abandoned couch, reading on her phone.

"Aren't you too excited to read your boring old book now?" Billie set down the glasses.

Ava's arm holding the phone dropped to her side like a felled branch. "I'm not reading my book," she said. "I just got another text from Bruno. He wants to talk."

CHAPTER 10

Ava closed the door to her bedroom and sat on her bed. She pulled up her legs and then put them down again. She leaned on the headboard and immediately decided it wasn't comfortable.

There was no being comfortable. Not when she had to tell Bruno that she wanted a divorce. It would never be comfortable until she got it over with.

Ava picked up her phone and pressed the speed dial. Bruno was still the number one.

"Ava!"

"Bruno?" She was almost startled at the fast response. Usually, he let her go to voice mail and called back at his convenience.

"Ava, where are you?"

"I'm in Mendocino Cove," she said. "I texted you."

"No, I know where... *Why* are you in Mendocino Cove?"

What was the best answer here? There were many things she could say, all of them complicated. "I needed to get away," Ava replied in the end.

"Why? Because of Ginny? Ava, I promise..." He inhaled deeply and audibly. "I promise there's nothing going on. I just need the help."

"No, not because of Ginny," Ava said carefully. "It's because you don't make time for me. You fill your hours with dictation and architecture and golfing, and there is no longer any space for me."

"What?"

"You haven't made room for me in years," Ava said. She felt hot, as if she had a fever. "In fact, you actively denied me space in your life. I've been little more than the domestic help, making sure your golf shirts are ironed."

"What are you talking about?"

"I'm talking about myself. I need to move on, Bruno. I want a divorce." She held her breath.

"A *divorce*?" He sounded confused.

"It must have occurred to you that our marriage is dead," Ava said. She didn't like the words. She had not expected to have to explain this part of it. In her mind, she needed only to tell him that her patience was at an end, and he would readily agree.

"I'm... Are you serious? What on earth got into you?"

"Are *you* serious? I truly can't tell whether you're joking."

"Ava...what brought this on?"

"I told you." Confusion flushed her cheeks. "I'm alone in our marriage. I have been for years, and I don't want to be lonely any longer. That's why I left. I didn't even think you'd notice."

"Of course I noticed." Bruno sounded impatient. "Why are you lonely?"

Ava shook her head. Was he being sincere? She had tried again and again to reach out to him before she gave up. "The kids are gone. You're golfing all day. I'm *alone*, Bruno. Every day, I'm alone in my house, with nothing to do but clean and shop and wait for a word from you. It's not how I want to live my life."

"I thought you had friends."

"I have friends. What I don't have is a *partner*."

"Come back. We can't talk about this on the phone. It's ridiculous."

Ava pressed her hand to her cheek. "I'm not coming back, Bruno," she said quietly. "And it's not ridiculous. One way or the other, I've brought this up countless times. You had years to change, but you didn't want to. I'm not coming back to tell you one more time, one more way. I'll do what's good for me now. I've been sad and confused for years. If you're sad and confused now...well, that's how it feels, I suppose, when a marriage falls apart."

"Where are you staying?" The words tumbled out so fast they blurred into each other.

"With a friend. But I'm buying a house."

"You're buying a *house*? Where?"

"My old childhood home in Mendocino Cove, actually, and I'm using my parents' money. The house is falling down, but I'm going to fix it up. And then I'm going to live in it, Bruno," Ava said. "I'm sorry things went this way. I've been sorry about it for years. I have to move on, and I hope you understand. But if you don't...well, I had to find my way through this mess on my own too. Maybe Ginny can help you. Or golfing. I don't know, and I don't have enough energy left to obsess on your behalf. Bye, Bruno."

"But do you still love me? Ava? Ava?"

"Love?" Ava pressed a fist against the space between her eyebrows. "I've always *loved* you, Bruno. But I want to be happy too." She exhaled, and then she gently lowered the phone and ended the call.

The phone dropped on the bed. Her hand was shaking. Suddenly, she had no idea how the call had gone. Good? Bad? Had she made sense? Had *he* made sense?

Why had he asked if she still loved him?

Why, after all these years of leaving her, had he asked about love?

A light knock on the door startled her.

"Yes?"

The door opened just enough for Billie's face to appear. "Everything okay?"

"Come in."

Billie came and sat on the bed beside Ava. "How did it go?"

She shook her head. "It was...weird. It was weird."

"Okay. How was it weird?"

"Good question." Ava thought about what exactly had made the call so strange. "I honestly expected we were on the same page," she said finally. "I thought he wanted to get divorced."

"Did he not?"

"I have no idea." She shrugged, feeling helpless. "I thought we'd just meet and pull out a calculator to divide the money. But he seemed so surprised. Like he didn't see it coming."

"Was he acting? It's possible that he doesn't want to divide the money."

"I don't really know him anymore. Was he acting? But why?"

"Maybe he still loves you," Billie said softly.

"Maybe I'm a commodity to him," Ava said. "Maybe it's inconvenient for him if I don't run the household."

"Do you still love him?"

"Yes. How can I not? I'm angry, and I'm resentful, and I'm lonely. But I've known him too long. How can you not love a person you've known for so many years?"

"That's not too hard, actually," Billie said wryly. "I know a few people who just don't seem to grow closer to my heart. My own ex, for example. The longer we were together, the less I liked him."

"That's not how I feel. I've just given up that *he* loves me back. I've accepted that I'm all alone in this marriage."

"Oh, honey." Billie reached over and pulled Ava into a hug. "You don't have to be alone any longer. We got you. Go ahead and get divorced if there's no hope he'll treat you with more respect. Or, you know..." She let the sentence trail off.

"What?" Ava straightened so she could see her friend's face. "Or what?"

"Or invite him here. Talk with him. Now that you've brought out the big D, it might open his eyes."

"I didn't do it lightly. I've thought about it for years before I made the call, and now I mean it. I'm going to go through with it." Billie was on her side, but still, Ava felt defensive.

Billie patted her hand. "Exactly," she said. "That is exactly why it has the power to open his eyes finally."

She took a shuddering breath. "What if he doesn't agree?"

"Does he have to? I think in this day and age, if you really want a divorce, you can have one."

"What did you do?" Ava asked.

Billie opened her eyes wide to show that her case had been entirely different. "I had all the reasons I needed. The judge practically threw the signed papers at me."

"Did he cheat?" Ava asked carefully.

"He did," Billie said. "Let's not talk about me. I'm happy."

"Are you never lonely?"

Billie shrugged. "What can I do? The only men I know are either my relatives or they are dating my friends. I just never meet anyone."

"That can't be true."

"I never meet anyone I *like*," Billie corrected herself.

CHAPTER 11

Jenny threw a careful glance at her daughter. Audrey—with bed hair, wearing a sleep shirt that said 'sass lives here' and fluffy slippers—was standing in the kitchen, drinking coffee and looking out of the window.

As far as Jenny could tell, Audrey was staring straight at the century-old cypress growing at the side of the house, seeing nothing.

Of course, Michael didn't need another waitress. He had found out that his only help at the Mermaid Galley, Hannah, ran a food truck after hours. Still, he'd offered Audrey wine and mussels and garlic bread, but no job.

As if she'd felt her mother's eyes on her back, Audrey turned around.

"You look great, Mom." She set her coffee mug down and ran her fingers through her hair. Then she smiled. "You'll have a blast teaching at the university. You'll be great at it too."

"Thank you, darling." Jenny tugged nervously on her shirt. Her outfit consisted of a simple white button-up and straight-cut khaki slacks the sales lady had sworn struck a balance between traditional and modern. "I can't tell you how nervous I am. What if the students don't like me?"

"Half our professors didn't like *us*." Audrey grinned. "So don't worry about it. Just tell them what you have to say and get back here to tell me how it went."

"Sage advice." Jenny smiled back.

"Would you like some coffee, Mom? Or a cinnamon bun? They're almost ready." Audrey had found a new passion in baking. It had reared its pretty head when she couldn't shake her East Coast jet lag and joined Jon in the kitchen in the early mornings.

They'd chatted and drank coffee, and little by little, Jon had let Audrey take over this and that baking task as he prepared his splendid breakfast feasts. Audrey was learning fast, and she loved not only the baking itself, but the part where her creations made people happy.

Usually, the cinnamon buns she offered would have made Jenny's stomach rumble, and the rich, warm, buttery smell of sweet carbs would have her waiting, plate in hand, in front of the oven.

But today, her stomach was engaging in all sorts of interesting gymnastics. For a moment, her thoughts flew to poor Faye.

She held up her hand. "Don't talk about food, darling. I'm queasy."

Audrey came over and hugged her, squeezing tightly. "You'll do great, Mom. They'll love you, but remember that they don't have to love you on the first day. Big breath. Just go in, say your piece, and get out."

Jenny wrapped her arms around her daughter. "I will. I will. I will. I could throw up; I'm so nervous."

Laughing, Audrey wiggled free. "All right, off you go. It's probably better if you just get started with the entire process instead of thinking about it. You're building it into something in your mind that it's probably not."

"The trick lies in that little word, *probably*," Jenny said. "But you're right, as always. Bye, sweetie." She kissed Audrey's forehead and turned to leave.

"Mom!"

"What?" Already at the front door, Jenny stopped. "What's wrong?"

"Nothing's wrong. You forgot your water bottle." Audrey brought her the bottle, then opened the door for her. "See you later, crocodile."

"In a while, alligator," Jenny said vaguely and stepped into the warm sunshine of a beautiful day. After the gray sky and almost rain of the night, it was nice not to have morning fog. She was already so tense that she shivered, even though she knew it was only her nerves and the prospect of public speaking.

She got in her car, couldn't find her keys, then found them and immediately dropped them again into the gap between her seat and the gear box. Cursing under her breath, she fished them out, over-bending one of her short, natural fingernails in the process and creating a blood-red crescent in the nail bed.

Waving her hurt hand at Audrey, she finally started the car. Moments later, she pulled from Forgotten Lane onto Main and was merrily on her way.

Not merrily. Stressed. Jenny blew an errant hair away that tickled her eyelid and swerved to avoid a bird swooping from a tree onto the road.

She hadn't worked when she was married, at least not for a salary. She had raised Audrey and River through all the different phases and years, had kept the house in order as best she could, had cooked and cleaned and maintained the family's social network. It had been hard and challenging at times.

But she rarely had to step up in front of a crowd and tell them things. Maybe once or twice at the PTA. Once in River's middle school orientation meeting, to declare who her hero was, because for some reason it had been a hero-oriented orientation.

Now, Jenny's class had twenty-five students. She'd stared at the number again last night, every second bringing more sweat to her palms.

These weren't preschoolers she could amuse with glue and glitter.

These were grown, intelligent, young people in the last throes of puberty and the first woes and glories of living in dorms with same-aged strangers.

The road swerved, and the Pacific Ocean opened in front of her. The sun had risen above the horizon, casting a bright glow on the sparkling water that reflected back the azure blue of the cloudless sky. The rugged cliffs were crowned with flowers and skirted with crashing waves, and suddenly, Jenny's worries seeped away like water in sand.

"Okay," she whispered, flicking her blinker and entering Maytown. "I can do this. I can totally do this."

Her phone rang, and she pressed the steering wheel control to answer. "Hey, Jon." She exhaled and felt better.

"Hi, beauty. Good morning. How are you?"

"Nervous until a second ago. I'm almost there."

"I don't want to say good luck because you got this and don't need luck. But...good luck, honey."

Honey. She smiled. "Thank you."

"I'll meet you at the hotel when you're done?"

"If you can, Jon. I know you have to work."

"The nice thing about grapes is that they grow themselves. I'll bring lunch."

"Thanks. You're..." She was going to say *the best.* But he was better than the best. "You're the love of my life, Jon."

"Hmm. I should've stayed over last night after all," he said in that low, seductive way that made the hairs on her neck stand up.

"I had to get some sleep." She laughed. "Tonight, we celebrate."

"Oh, yes, we will."

"All right, my turn is coming up. Kisses," Jenny said and stopped at the traffic light.

"You got this. You know what to say, you know where to go. See you soon." Jon hung up.

The light turned, and Jenny pulled into the parking lot of Elizabeth May University. Her heart was starting to beat its way into her throat again when she parked in the small faculty lot.

"Just ignore it," she whispered to herself when she turned off the engine. "Ignore. Ignore." She wasn't going to let the butterflies and their whopping big wings win. The best thing she could do was to march into that lecturing hall cool and collected, exuding knowledge and natural authority.

Jenny grabbed her phone and got out, automatically pressing her finger into the groove on the handle to lock the car.

She knew where the classroom was. She knew what she was going to talk about. She knew... She'd forgotten what she knew. Oh, right, homework... She had written down a homework assignment for the students.

What was it again? Jenny stopped walking toward the building. Her palms were sweatier than ever. The assignment was written on the notepad, together with her notes.

And the notepad was...in the car. Also, the water bottle.

She frowned and speed-marched back. She was wasting the time she had planned in for finding the classroom and trying out the computer system, making sure the speaker worked, and making sure she owned the turf before the students came in.

But she couldn't afford many more trips back and forth across the parking lot because she was too nervous to remember her things.

She slid her hand around the car handle, which usually made the car automatically unlock itself. But this time, there was no clicking sound.

Jenny pulled on the handle and tried the motion again.

Nothing.

The notes were sitting on the passenger seat, exactly where she'd put them.

So were the car keys.

CHAPTER 12

The car Jenny and Audrey had bought together was lovely. It was sturdy, and newish, and it did convenient tricks like locking and unlocking the door when you touched the handle in certain ways.

What it didn't know, unfortunately, was not to lock the door when the key was still inside. It seemed an obvious feature to give a car.

Jenny blinked a few times.

Maybe the makers thought people should have free will. If they wanted to lock themselves out right before giving their first lecture ever, sure. Go ahead. Knock yourselves out. It's a free country.

The sound that came out of Jenny's mouth sounded like a cross between a frustrated gull's squawk and the hiss of a stalking lynx.

For a moment, she considered calling Jon. Audrey had the second key. He could bring it in twenty minutes.

But she wouldn't make it in time for the lecture. One thing Jenny knew was that she had to set an example for the students. Being punctual was more important than handing out homework.

As for the rest of her notes...that was a bummer. She threw a last, longing glance at them. Without them, she would have to wing it using only the slides in her Power-Point presentation. She'd spent a long time putting it together; she would remember what she meant to say if she could just calm down. Right now, it seemed to be a big if...

"Dr. Summers?"

Jenny's head jerked up. That was her—she was Dr. Summers! "Yes?" She looked around.

"To your left. It's Angela—the department secretary?"

"Oh yes, of course. Hi, Angela. Please call me Jenny. Nobody has ever called me Dr. Summers."

Angela smiled politely. "Can I help you? You look lost."

"I locked my notes in," Jenny confessed shamefacedly. "How is that for a first day?"

Angela was supposed to laugh or at least smile. Instead, she looked even more serious. "Do you need them to give your lecture? If you are going to be late, I should tell the students."

Jenny suppressed a sigh. She wasn't here to be funny. She was here to teach the department's students. She was supposed to be a professional, someone the department could trust. "No," she said quickly. "It's fine. I meant to bring them, but it doesn't matter."

Angela nodded. "I'm glad I caught you, Dr. Summers. Would you mind swapping your classroom for one of the lecture halls? Dr. Kendall wanted two video screens today, and your classroom is the only one that has two. It's only this one time. She'd be grateful if you could help her out."

"Of course." Jenny cleared her throat. One of the big lecture halls? They fit hundreds of students, and she had all of twenty-five. This wasn't going according to plan at all.

For the first time, Angela's smile reached her eyes. "Thanks," she said. "Then you'll be in 307 West."

"Right. Where is that?"

"One up, to the left, last glass door by the bathrooms, left, left, and then it's the large double door." Angela nodded. "I have to run and buy coffee for the department's coffee maker. You good?"

"Yes, thank you. I'm good," Jenny confirmed weakly. She'd already forgotten the directions. "307 West," she whispered so she wouldn't forget that too, and then she started to walk to the building. Never mind notes and homework and happy students. If she could only find the correct room now, she'd be content.

The small university had one of the prettiest campuses Jenny could imagine. Situated on a bluff, it overlooked the ocean that peeked out from between the old brick buildings. Mature rhododendrons carrying a profusion of white and purple flowers competed for space with tall oak trees that shaded the walkways crisscrossing the lawn and connecting the buildings.

Jenny found her way to the one housing the history department, pushed open the heavy glass door, and entered. Inside, it was cool, and the air smelled of coffee and paper and floor wax. She hurried past glass cases full of anthropological and historical treasures and stopped at the staircase.

This was the east wing. Wasn't it? The sea was in the west. But neither staircase led closer to the sea. In fact, they seemed to be north and south wings. Jenny tried another staircase, but it only led to the math department.

She checked her phone. Ten minutes to go. Through the open doors, she could see into the classrooms she was passing. Students already filled the seats, their legs outstretched, scrolling on their phones.

"Excuse me," she whispered and waved at a professor in a bright, airy classroom with big windows.

He was writing equations on the board with scratchy chalk. "Yes?" He raised an eyebrow but didn't come to the door.

Jenny inhaled. "I'm looking for Room 307 West," she said desperately. "I'm a new adjunct in the history department."

Now he smiled and joined her at the door. "It's right around the corner. Go down those stairs, and then you're practically in front of it." He pointed. "The really big doors."

"Thank you," she whispered, gratitude washing through her, and hurried on.

There it was. She pushed open the door and stopped short.

A massive, dark lecture hall sprawled ahead of her. Nothing like the friendly, sunny rooms in the math department, this hall was meant to house half the university. The staggered rows of seats that bend in a sickle shape around the lectern would seat two or even three hundred people.

And every single seat was empty.

No students with outstretched legs scrolling on phones.

Jenny wished she had her notes, just so she could hold on to them. She couldn't see a light switch, so she propped the door open for light. Slowly, she made her way to the lectern. Where was the computer? Where was the screen?

"Five minutes to showtime," she whispered. "I have no idea what to do here."

Suddenly, the lights came on. Jenny blinked and looked up, startled.

"Jenny? It's Carolina." The woman standing in the door on top of the amphitheater was Dr. Perez, the head of the history department. She and Jenny had become friends over the last weeks, and an angel couldn't have been more welcome.

"Carolina!"

"Hey there," Carolina said. "I told them not to put you in here on the first day, but do you think they will listen?"

"Carolina, help me," Jenny said, the words tumbling from her mouth. "Where is the computer?"

"Did nobody—" Shaking her head, Carolina came down the stairs. "It's in here." She opened the tiny cupboard under the lectern and pressed a button on the small desktop computer tucked under there. Then she went to the wall and pressed another button, and a huge screen hummed down in front of a whiteboard that spanned the width of the room. "Here." Carolina set a mouse on the lectern and handed Jenny a remote. "Use it to click through your slides."

"Okay."

"Do you have everything you need? I have to run to a meeting."

"Well—where are the students?"

"Good question. Uh. Remember, they're freshmen. They'll be extra confused because the rooms were switched. You get ready for them. I'll call Mimi and make sure she sends them over."

"Who?"

"Mimi Kendall. She's a professor in the anthropology department. You swapped rooms with her, and I bet she's trying to sort out her students from yours right now."

"Thanks, Carolina," Jenny said. "I guess I'll just stay here and hope they'll come."

"That's what we all do," Carolina waved and ran, quite literally, out of the room to get to her meeting.

At least Jenny had the memory stick with her PowerPoint lecture in her pocket. She wiggled it into the computer slot. Her files showed up larger than life on the board. Hastily, she clicked to where she needed to be, opening a photo of one of Nantucket's famous houses covered in tumbling roses.

Jenny sat down on the bottom step of the steep aisle that ran from the lectern to the top row to wait for her students.

"There once was a whale in Nantucket," she whispered to keep herself company. "Who almost fit in a bucket. It is too small, said the whaler appalled. Let's call it a day and say—"

"Hey. Is this Lost at Sea: Shipwrecks and Maritime Mysteries of Nantucket?"

Startled, Jenny looked up. A young face looked down at her from the door by the top aisle. Quickly, she stood. "Yes."

Another young face appeared, this one male. "Are you the prof?" he asked suspiciously.

"Yes. I am." Jenny hoped there was no dust on the bottom of her slacks. "Come on in."

The girl pointed over her shoulder. "Only because we thought it was in the other room. We're so confused."

"It's all right." Jenny smiled. "I was confused too. Come on in and find a seat."

"Okay." The two trudged in, never looking at her again, and found seats in the top row. As far away from her as they possibly could be.

More and more students followed until the whole twenty-five of them were there. Not filling the vast hall by far, they perched in the farthest row like frightened hens in the cargo area of a Victorian whaling ship. Only one boy with glasses and slicked-back hair came down the stairs. His face was arranged into a careful mask saying, *I don't care if they laugh*, and he sat down right in front of Jenny.

She looked at him, and then she looked up at the rest of her students.

The door fell shut with a creak, and the only light came from the glowing PowerPoint slide.

"Is that where you are going to sit?" she asked after a while.

"What?" the first girl said. "Can you talk louder? We can't hear you."

"*I* can hear you," the single student in front of her said. "It's loud enough for *me*."

"Okay." Jenny turned to the screen, then remembered the maybe dusty bottom of her slacks and turned again.

Figuring the start was always hardest, Jenny had carefully thought about the first words she would say.

Ladies and gentlemen, fellow enthusiasts of maritime history, today I have the distinct pleasure of delivering a lecture on a subject deeply intertwined with the heritage and legacy of Nantucket—the captivating tale of whaling. Join me as we embark on a voyage through time to explore the rich whaling history of this enchanting island and the profound impact it had on Nantucket's development.

Jenny cleared her throat. That introduction was never going to fly. Not in a million years.

"All right," she said out loud. "Let's talk about Nantucket, a little island on the East Coast. Nowadays, it's a really pretty tourist destination. But not so long ago, Nantucket was full of whalers."

"What do you mean, whalers?" the student in front of her asked.

"A whaler is someone who hunts whales," Jenny replied.

"It's *wrong* to hunt whales."

"Yeah! That's bull!" someone yelled from the top row, and several girls giggled.

"Oooh boy," Jenny whispered under her breath, and then she straightened her shoulders and clapped her hands. "All right, everyone, leave your bags in your seats. Let's go outside and sit in the grass on the bluff so we can see the ocean. We need to think about reasons why the good people of Nantucket would have chosen to hunt whales."

CHAPTER 13

Faye slid the pregnancy test across her kitchen table to Billie and pressed a fist on the tight line of her lips. Whether to keep herself from screaming, from throwing up, or both, she couldn't tell.

The morning after the dinner at the vineyard, Jenny had dropped off the test as promised. For two days, Faye had stared at it, working up the courage to actually use it. It was okay to wonder whether she was pregnant. *Knowing* was a whole different ball game.

"That's a second line all right," Billie said in a wavering voice. "That's a big blue yes, Faye."

"Jenny bought two. They both show the same." Faye sucked in a shaky breath. "I haven't told her yet because she's teaching today."

"Okay. Okay. No reason to panic. So you're pregnant. Uh. Yay?" Billie leaned across the table, reached out, and pulled the fist from Faye's mouth. Then she sat back, uncurling Faye's fingers and holding them between her hands. "Don't panic. What are you feeling?"

"I'm too *old*," it broke from Faye. She pulled her chin back, surprised. Among the tidal wave of concerns she'd had after the first shock settled, her age had not been at the forefront.

"Okay."

"What do you mean, okay?" Faye's heartbeat was like a prancing racehorse. It tossed its head and bolted here and there in her chest cavity, doing anything but plodding steadily ahead. "Okay means bad, right?"

"No."

"No? Then why don't you say it doesn't matter?"

"Breathe, Faye. I'm trying to acknowledge your feelings. I read in a magazine that's what we're supposed to do."

"But I don't want you to acknowledge I'm too old! I want you to say it's going to be fine!" Faye's breath left her lungs explosively, leaving her coughing. It was like every part of her body had decided to take matters into their own hands now.

It was understandable. If she couldn't protect her womb, why would her stomach, heart, or lungs want to do what she wanted?

"Calm down. Calm, calm," Billie said, as if Faye was one of her rescue pelicans.

"I'm calm." Faye's upper lip shook, and she pulled it between her teeth.

"Listen. You're fine. Women in their forties have babies all the time."

"What if I'm so old it has a genetic defect?"

"Then we deal with it, Faye. Listen to me—do not snowball. It's not good for you or for the baby."

Faye's knees felt weak. The baby. The baby. She was going to have a *baby*. "It feels unreal," she whispered.

"Before I came over, I called a friend of mine who's a nurse in Redwood Hospital. She said there was a cancellation with her favorite obstetrician today, and she penciled you in. We'll go, okay? I'm coming with you."

Faye took a deep breath. She'd hopped on a one-way train, and there was no getting off the tracks now. "Okay," she said faintly. "When?"

Billie checked her watch. "We should leave in an hour. Let's get you showered and dressed. Are you sure you don't want any breakfast? Not even toast?"

Faye let her gaze graze the breakfast table. For once, Billie had stuck to the bland basics—toast, oatmeal with honey, fruit salad.

She shook her head and turned to go take her shower. In the door, she stopped and turned. "Billie—thank you. I appreciate your help. I know I'm being difficult."

"Please," Billie said comfortably and spooned almond butter and strawberry jam on her toast. "I've been there. From now on, everything is just a phase. Give it eighteen years or so for things to smooth over."

Faye pressed a hand to her mouth because the smell of her normally beloved almond butter hit wrong. There was barely time to nod before she had to race to the bathroom.

The shower helped to settle her upset stomach. Or maybe the nausea had just run its course; the waves followed their own fancy. By the time she was drying herself with an abundance of fluffy towels, Faye felt perfectly fine.

She turned in front of the mirror to see her stomach from the side. There was not a thing to see. Was it really real? A real baby? Her own? To keep?

Strong morning sickness was a good sign, according to the internet. So, just maybe...maybe everything would be fine? Maybe sometime next spring, she'd bring home a cute, healthy little baby boy or girl?

Every thought attached to the baby came with a question mark.

Faye slipped into loose sweats and a wide T-shirt. Usually she wouldn't go out dressed like that. The hope was that the obstetrician realized that cashmere and morning sickness weren't compatible.

After she dried her hair, pulled it into a bun on top of her head, put on makeup and diamond earrings to make up for the sloppy outfit, there was nothing more to do. Faye squeezed a squirt of hand cream out of the bottle and rubbed it in.

Billie knocked on the door. "Are you ready? We should go."

"Coming." Faye gave herself one last look. Her reflection looked back, worried and pinched.

"Faye?"

"Yeah." She unlocked the bathroom door.

Billie was waiting outside, her leather purse slung over her shoulder. "Grab your health insurance card and let's go do this," she said. "They won't bite. I promise."

"I know they don't bite. I'm worried *I'll* bite," Faye said wryly and went to get her own purse from the closet. "All right. I'm good right now. Let's try to get there before the nausea comes back."

"Uh-oh." Billie looked alarmed. "Let's go."

Billie drove out to the hospital.

They'd visited there when Harry Donovan passed away. Faye had once been engaged to Harry's son, Lex, and even though they broke up, old man Donovan left Faye the money to pay off her house on Cormorant Lane.

That was going to be helpful now that she would be a single mom with a baby.

"You haven't told Gabe yet, have you?" Billie asked as she parked in the hospital's visitor lot. "I mean, I know you haven't because I'm sure if you had, he would be driving you right now."

"I don't want to tell him until I'm one hundred per-cent sure." Faye got out of the car. The sun was bright today, and despite the early hour, it was about four hundred degrees already. She wiped the sweat from her temples.

Billie waited for Faye to join her. Together, they start-ed walking to the hospital. "How do you think he'll react?"

Faye shook her head. At the mention of Gabe, her heart tossed its mane and started prancing sideways into the carefully tended flower beds of her lungs. She pressed a hand to her sternum to calm it. "We've been dating for a few weeks, Billie," she said. "I honestly don't know. Maybe if we'd been dating for six months or a year, I'd be more confident in making a prediction." She pulled open the door to the hospital and was immediately assaulted by the smell of antiseptic and floor wax and the flowers in the tiny gift shop.

Billie glanced at her. "I think he'll be over the moon," she said, but the words lacked conviction.

"Yeah, maybe," Faye said, also lacking conviction.

Gabe was great. She was in love with him, no doubt about it. But you didn't learn in a handful of weeks everything there was to know about a person. They had never talked about marriage. They had certainly never talked about babies, let alone having one with *each other*.

"I think this will be very unexpected for him," she said as they signed in and then climbed the stairs to the OB/GYN's office. "Like it was for me."

Billie opened the last door. "You guys weren't careful," she whispered. "Gabe definitely knows how babies are made, so maybe it's not as unexpected as you think."

Faye bit her lip. It had occurred to her too. But after forty-three years of not getting pregnant, the risk had seemed so abstract. Like there was a big note over her head, reading, *please excuse Faye McAllister from getting pregnant because she's been lucky so far.*

"Hi, Billie." The woman at the reception smiled at them.

"Hi, Pam." Billie pointed at Faye.

"So you're Faye?" Pam nodded.

"I am." Faye's throat was dry.

"Nice to meet you. I'm Pamela. Can I see your insurance card while you fill this in?"

Faye obediently handed over the little plastic card and took the clipboard with the check-in papers.

"Thanks for squeezing us in so quickly, Pam," Billie said.

"You bet. You got lucky that a lady canceled her appointment right before you called. We're pretty booked out."

Faye filled out her papers and returned them to Pamela, who competently pointed out a signature Faye had missed and then tapped even more competently on her keyboard.

Faye looked at the other ladies in the waiting room. One, hugely pregnant already, was holding hands with her clearly besotted husband, who couldn't stop touching her belly. Another woman sat alone, legs crossed and studiously avoiding anyone's gaze. A third was there with a two-year-old who spun like a top in tight circles. It made Faye dizzy just to watch.

"Faye?"

Faye looked at Billie, who patted her arm.

"Good luck," Billie whispered. "I'll be right here."

Faye followed the nurse and had barely changed into a paper gown and sat down on the one chair that wasn't the doctor's stool or the exam table when a Korean lady in pink slacks and a buttoned-up white lab coat entered.

"Hello, Miss McAllister. I'm Doctor Pak," she said and flipped through Faye's registration papers. "So, you think you are pregnant?" She looked up and smiled the warmest smile Faye had ever seen.

"I had a positive test. Uh—it wasn't entirely planned. I mean—" She hugged herself. "It was entirely *not* planned."

"Huge shock?" Somehow, the smile got even warmer.

"You could say that." Faye took a shuddering breath.

"I promise you're not the first one."

"It's not that I don't want it." The words surprised her almost as much as the positive test. But once they were out there, hovering in the air between her and the doctor, she knew they were true.

Faye did want her little baby girl or boy. She *wanted* it. Some gate inside her broke open. "I do want it," she said out loud, tasting the words. "I want the baby."

"And if everything goes according to plan, you shall have it." Dr. Pak tapped the computer's keyboard, and the screen flickered to life. "All right, let's see here. When was the first day of your last period?"

"I have no idea. I quit writing it down years ago."

Dr. Pak grinned over her shoulder at Faye. "This pregnancy is going to be lots of fun for you."

Faye grinned back. "Let's try another question."

"No, let's not." Dr. Pak handed Faye a calendar. "This one's kind of a biggie."

Faye shook her head. "Could have been here." She tapped a date. "No, wait. Here." She tapped another. "No. That can't be right."

"Okay." Dr. Pak pulled on gloves and clapped her hands. "Up on the chair we go. If I don't get my answers one way, I'll get them another."

Chapter 14

Ava walked to the red cast-iron mailbox in front of Billie's seaside cottage, letting her fingers trail over the fragrant flowers that held their faces to the late morning sun.

She would have quite liked to be included in whatever it was her old friends were cooking up, but Billie had declared that it was something she and Faye had to do on their own.

It was fair enough. Jenny, Faye, and Billie were like sisters. But even a sister couldn't expect to be always included after falling out of touch for so many years.

A single blue envelope lay in the mailbox. Ava pulled it out and flipped it over. It was addressed to her. Her eyes flicked to the return sticker. The letter was from her husband.

Bruno had written her a *letter*.

Or maybe he dictated it to Ginny...

Ava sighed. She didn't like that her thoughts immediately landed on Ginny. Bruno had sounded sincere when he said there was nothing going on between them. She wanted to believe him. She wanted to preserve that small part of her that trusted him.

Ava took the letter and went to the dock, where she sat at the table. The coast here was protected by a cliff that broke the waves and funneled calmer water into a cove. Still, it was breezy, and the dock swayed lightly under her feet. She tucked her flying hair back and then opened the letter.

Dear Ava,

As I sit down to write this letter, my heart is heavy with regret and sadness. I know that things between us have not been good lately and that I have been a part of the problem. I want you to know that I love you and that I miss you more than I, and maybe you too, could have imagined.

I won't deny that your disappearance left me baffled, and that I was angry after you hung up on me when I called. How could you buy a house without letting me know?

I sat with a bottle of wine in the garden and thought about everything you said. I know I started out thinking you were being unfair, and this was coming out of the blue. But the longer I thought about it, the more I replayed our past conversations in my head, the more the fog lifted.

Maybe both of us could have communicated better, maybe not. When I got up from that chair in the garden, I could see that I had made mistakes in our marriage. I promised to protect and love and honor you. Instead, I caused you pain and hurt.

For that, I am truly sorry. I never meant to hurt you. I think when the kids were little and we weren't paying attention, life picked us up and tossed us in different directions. I want you to know that I am committed to making things right between us and that I will do whatever it takes to earn back your trust and your love.

Ava let the blue paper sink and looked at the water. He apologized. And he still loved her?

She wanted to believe in Bruno's words, but she had been hurt for too long. For years, his actions spoke for themselves. One night in a garden could change things, but could it change a workaholic who outsourced his happiness from his home to the golf course?

"Pretty words," she whispered.

And yet, that small part of her that still believed? It grew a little.

She folded the page and slid it back into the envelope. Then she pulled out the second and last page and tucked the envelope under her leg so it wouldn't fly away.

Maybe she should get a bottle of wine too, she thought as she unfolded the page.

You are the love of my life, and I cannot imagine my future without you in it. You are the light in my darkest moments, the laughter in my happiest times, and the one who has always been there for me, no matter what. I miss your touch, your smile, and the sound of your voice.

Ava frowned. He missed her *touch*? Had Ginny written this for him? She couldn't remember the last time they'd touched. Not even casually, like a goodnight hug.

But did that mean he didn't miss it?

I know that it will take time and effort to rebuild what we have lost, but I am willing to do that. I want to show you that I love you and that I'm committed to making things right between us.

Please come back to me, Ava. Give me another chance to make things right between us, and I promise you that I will spend the rest of my life making sure that you know how much I care.

Forever and always,

Your Bruno

"Okay," she murmured and let the letter sink. "That's a lot of pretty words and pretty sentiments."

She slid the page into the envelope and tucked it back under her leg. Then she crossed her arms and wiggled her foot up and down as she thought.

It was a nice letter. No doubt. Bruno had properly apologized. That was a lot, even if he shared the blame for the rift in their relationship between them. He didn't admit to more, but it took two to tango. Ava had shut down at some point, no longer trying to salvage things. She could acknowledge that.

Everything else he wrote just seemed so unlikely. If Bruno loved her so much, surely she would have felt it? Ava hadn't imagined feeling lonely and isolated in her marriage. The neglect had been real.

She picked up her phone and dialed his number.

"Ava. I'm so glad you called."

"Hi, Bruno. I just read your letter."

He cleared his throat. "And?"

"I appreciate the apology and the insight. But I have a hard time believing you really miss me." Ava's voice sounded incredulous even to herself. "You miss my touch? Really?"

"Yes, really. I've missed it for a long time."

"You could have touched me. I was right there, every night. Beside you, wanting to cry because you turned your back to me."

"You wanted to cry? I thought you didn't want *me*. You turned away too."

"I was tired of initializing. I was tired of begging for affection."

He groaned. "Ava...I had no idea."

Ava sighed. "I'm not coming back, Bruno. I want to believe everything you wrote to me and are saying, but I don't. I can't."

"But where does that leave me? What if I am sincere, Ava? Don't I deserve a second chance?"

"You've had your chance, Bruno. We both have used up all our chances."

There was a long silence. "Where are you right now?" he finally asked.

Ava's heart dropped. He hadn't paid attention when she told him where she was? How stupid of her to let a letter lift her hopes. "In Mendocino Cove." Disappointment muffled her voice.

"No, I know you're in Mendocino Cove, at your friend Billie's," he said. "I sent you a letter there, didn't I?"

"Then why do you ask?" It was true—he had sent her a letter. For a moment, Ava was ashamed for being so suspicious.

"I want to picture you. Are you outside? Is there traffic? I hear rushing."

"I'm by the sea."

"Oh. Where? On a beach?"

She tilted her head. It was more than he'd wanted to know about her in a long while. "Actually, I'm sitting on a large dock. There's a table where Billie and her friends like to have breakfast. They're gone now, but that's where I'm sitting."

"You are alone?"

"I wouldn't call you to talk about these things if I weren't alone."

"Ava." He paused. "Do you have to be so snappy?"

She exhaled. "I don't trust you anymore. I used to. But it evaporated over the long years of trying to connect with you and not succeeding."

"What can I do to make you trust me again? What does it take to win *you* back?"

Ava shrugged instinctively. "I don't know," she admitted. "I feel like I crossed the point of no return."

"How is the house sale going?" he said after a moment of silence.

"Good, I think," she said, surprised. "It takes time to sort out the paperwork, but things are rolling along. The handover should be soon."

"Okay. Take care of yourself, will you?"

"Yes." She swallowed. So this was it. This was the end of their marriage. "You too, Bruno. You might not believe me—but I truly do love you."

"I know. I love you too. Bye."

"Bye."

A click in the line told Ava that her husband had hung up.

She put her head on the backrest, pulled out the rubber band holding her bun, and shook out her hair. Free. She was free.

Ava closed her eyes. The sun shone warm on her face, and the sea rushed a song.

His pretty words hadn't meant anything after all. The next letter in her mailbox would not be from Bruno. It would be from his lawyer.

Unbidden tears started to drip from her eyes. She wiped them away. "Don't be silly," she whispered. "Stop. Stoppit."

But the tears didn't stop. They kept dripping down from the corners of her eyes, down her temples and into her hairline, until she straightened again. Then they dripped down her cheek and her nose and her chin, leaving cool trails on her sun-warmed face.

CHAPTER 15

Jenny stretched her arms, glad to be where she was. They had decided it was time for a girls' picnic lunch, and she was sitting with Faye, Ava, and Billie on blankets on the rocks by the sea where they used to play together so many years ago. They had picked a spot toward the land, where the rocks were flat and wide and the shade of an ancient cypress protected them. As kids, they'd eaten PBJ's here in shorts and T-shirts. But on this day, they had brought baskets and coolers and blankets, climbing over the rocks in straw hats and fluttering sun dresses.

Jenny had brought china and crystal and blankets from the hotel, Billie brought sandwiches with prosciutto, cheese, and truffle cream, Faye brought cheese and crackers and grapes, and Ava had brought orange juice and prosecco for mimosas and stayed up late the night before to make her special tiramisu.

"We need to catch up with each other," Billie declared and refilled their flutes. "Have another sandwich, Faye."

"Don't mind if I do. They taste like heaven."

"I agree. I want to know what's happening with everyone." Jenny glanced at Faye's flute. She was pretty sure that the orange juice in Faye's glass was just that. Orange juice.

Jenny took a sip of her own, happily spiked, mimosa.

Faye stuffed the last of her sandwich into her mouth, chewed, and swallowed. "I have an announcement."

Jenny lowered her glass and moved expectantly so the sunshine didn't prevent her from seeing Faye's face.

"I'm pregnant," Faye said.

Jenny smiled. Billie winked at her.

"No!" Ava set her glass down. "No, you're not!"

"Yes, I am. Believe me when I say it was a surprise." Faye lifted her glass of juice. "Cheers."

"Congratulations?" Jenny asked and, like the other two, chinked her glass to Faye's.

"Yes. I'm getting used to the idea."

Ava smiled broadly. "Is Gabe over the moon?"

Billie popped a grape into her mouth. "Gabe doesn't know yet. We can't tell anyone, okay?"

"Sure."

"I haven't told him yet," Faye confessed and set down her glass. "I need to do it soon. I'm almost eight weeks along."

"You've only dated Gabe for about that long," Jenny mentioned. "Isn't that right?"

Faye groaned. "I swear it happened that very first time! Neither one of us was prepared."

"Are you excited?" Ava asked. "Or are you mostly stressed out since it wasn't planned?"

"I'm mostly *nauseated*," Faye said. "Though so far, today has been peachy."

"Maybe it's getting better," Jenny said cheerfully. "I remember it settling much later with Audrey, but maybe you get lucky—*again!*" She laughed. Innuendos would follow Faye for a while now.

"I sincerely hope so. The doctor gave me a list of foods that help the stomach. So far, so good. Knock on wood." She tapped her knuckles to a piece of sun-bleached driftwood.

"But honestly, Faye," Ava insisted. "Are you happy?"

"I'm getting there," Faye admitted. "All joking aside, I'm worried about Gabe's reaction. If it's as much of a shock for him as it was to me—who knows what he wants to do?"

"What do you want to do?" Billie asked.

"I want to keep it," Faye said slowly. "It's already my little baby daughter. Or son. I realized that when I was sitting in the waiting room of the doctor's office. Had Dr. Pak said I wasn't pregnant after all or something was wrong, it would have hit me hard."

"Obviously, she didn't say that," Jenny prodded. She wanted more information. It was hard not to picture what it would be like if she and Jon had a baby together.

She would love that child. Adore it.

But to have to start all over again? Diapers and first steps and sleepless nights, the forty endless years of middle school and the half-second flash that was high school...

"No, Dr. Pak didn't say that." Faye smiled. "She said everything looked okay and the due date will be next March."

"Wow. A little Faye baby." Billie shook her head.

"I hope Gabe will want to stay together," Faye confessed. "A baby is a lot of pressure on a relationship. We simply haven't been together long enough for me to predict what will happen."

"When are you going to tell him?" Ava asked.

"Soon," Faye said vaguely. She picked up a white sea shell, then tossed it into the nearby rock pool.

"Tomorrow?" Ava smiled. "It's just—now that my marriage is over, there are things I wish I'd done differently. Telling my husband more things sooner, whether or not he wanted to hear them, is one of them."

Faye took a deep breath and nodded. "Today. He wants to cook me dinner at his house. I'm already nervous. Girls—let's focus on someone else. Jenny, how was your first day at the university?"

"It was..." Jenny broke a cracker in two as she struggled for words. "Difficult. I think students have changed since the last time I taught."

"Tell us everything," Billie said and laid on her back, closing her eyes against the sun filtering through the branches of the cypress. "Start at the moment you pulled into the parking lot."

"It was truly a series of unfortunate events," Jenny said. "I was so nervous, I locked myself out of the car. My notes were still inside, of course."

"Oh, no." Faye and Ava laughed, and Billie smiled lazily.

"Then they put me in a lecture hall that swallowed my poor handful of students. I ended up overthrowing all my carefully laid plans and just taking them outside."

"That sounds nice," Ava remarked. "My profs would sometimes teach outside. I loved when that happened."

"My students did too," Jenny reported. "Which was my lucky break. I had prepared this fancy discourse on the economy of Nantucket, but a couple of them immediately swerved into a discussion of the ethics of hunting whales."

"Why?" Billie asked bluntly. "It was a long time ago."

"I guess it was on their minds." Jenny shrugged. "The entire class got caught up in the topic, and it's mostly what we talked about. At least it seemed like everyone had a good time, and I was able to weave a few facts about relevant history in there." She sighed. "Teaching is going to be an adventure. I can tell already."

Billie rolled on her side and propped her head in her hand. "Sounds like you did well. I had a prof once who couldn't deal with any changes to the plan. He'd just yell at us."

"I don't think that would have gone so well." Jenny chuckled at the thought. "We'll see how many of them come back next time. They can still drop the class if they want to."

"A concise summary," Billie said. "I like it. What's up in your life, Ava? Catch everyone up."

Ava cleared her throat. "I told my husband I want a divorce."

"For real? Did you mean it?" Faye asked, wide-eyed. One of her hands went to her flat stomach.

"I mean it."

"Well, don't leave us hanging." Jenny poured Ava another glass. "What did he do? What happened?"

"Nothing. Nothing really happened. He's not made time for me since before the kids left home. I thought things would change when he retired, but he just swapped the office for the golf course. He's still working too. Only now he's swinging the golf club while he's dictating his letters." She pressed her lips together.

"I'm not one to ask," Faye said. "But I assume you told him?"

"I did. Over the years, I told him everything."

"Have you told him all at once?" Billie asked. "With emphasis?"

"Uh." Ava scratched her chin. "You mean one big blowout? No, we've never had a proper fight. It was softer than that. I complained, and he slipped out of the house. Do you think a big fight would have worked?"

"I have no idea." Billie propped herself on her elbows. "I wasn't judging."

Ava looked down at her hands. "He wrote me a letter, saying he loved me. I was surprised to learn that he doesn't want a divorce."

"Men never want a divorce unless they have already found someone else," Billie said. "At least that's what I read on the internet."

"Qualified advice, then," Jenny said and shook her head at Billie. "How did the letter make you feel, Ava?"

She thought for a moment. "Like it was too good to be true. Like he was telling me what I wanted to hear."

"Do you still love him?" Faye asked eagerly.

"I will always love him," Ava said. "But I'm tired of being lonely. I'm tired of wondering about the state of our marriage. At some point, I need to acknowledge it's over. Don't I?"

"When it was over with Lex, it was *over*," Faye said. "I stopped loving him. It took a while to even *like* him after he left. I like him a lot more now that a few decades have passed. But I don't love him the way I love Gabe."

"Maybe it's different when you've been together for so many years," Ava said.

"I know what you mean," Jenny said suddenly. "My husband lied to me for a long time about the state of the business. But I still love him too. I would have tried to work things out if I'd had the chance."

"What about Jon?" Billie looked up.

Jenny smiled. "Jon is another story. It's not like I held them next to each other and picked the one I liked best."

"But if you would have met Jon again before you married Stan?" Billie insisted.

"I'd have chosen Jon," Jenny admitted. "I still love Stan, though."

"And you, Billie?" Ava asked.

"I don't understand this at all," she said cold-heart-edly. "I was glad when my divorce went through, and I didn't have to see his face anymore."

"Oof." Ava exhaled. "That rough, huh?"

Billie all but growled in answer.

Jenny had never gotten the full story of what had happened. She only knew that Billie had two grown sons whom Jenny had met only once, and then briefly, on the day of Harry Donovan's funeral. They seemed like nice kids, but they led busy lives in or near San Francisco. Jenny would have liked to know them better, and it would be good for Audrey to have company her own age. "What about your boys? I'd like to meet them again."

Billie smiled. "I'll call them tonight. We might actually have a window where they're both free."

Jenny nodded. Maybe someday soon she would take Billie aside and ask about her ex.

Her phone rang, and Jenny checked who it was. Then she said, "Excuse me, girls, I should take this." She stood, extracting herself carefully from the tangle of plates and legs and glasses on the blanket.

"Aunt Georgie," she said as she walked deeper into the shade. It was a hot day. Out in the heat, the aroma of the picnic foods mixed with that of deep, cool tidepools and the salty scent of the sea. Here in the shadows, where the light was green and brown and ocher, it smelled of wild rosemary.

"Jenny? Jenny, is that you?" Her aunt's voice was high-pitched and stressed.

"Yes, it's me. What's going on?" Jenny couldn't remember the last time her aunt had called her. Maybe it had been years ago since then. Jenny pressed a hand to her heart.

"I'm here on the...the cruise ship, and I'm hiding behind the lifeboat."

"Why? Why are you by the lifeboat? Is the ship sinking?"

"No," Aunt Georgie hissed. "No, but Klaus asked me to dance."

"I don't understand. Are you safe?"

"I'm—we had lunch and then he asked me to dance, and of course I went. It was a samba, very sexy, and people were having afternoon cocktails. You know how they are."

"I don't," Jenny said truthfully. "How are they?"

"Sweet and easy on the booze. But Klaus can't hold his liquor—not even a little bit. A minute into dancing, he got that look in his eyes."

Jenny took a centering breath. "What look?

"Like he wanted to spend the rest of his life with me. Like he was going to pull a big rock out of his pocket and slip it on my finger."

"You think he's going to propose to you?" Jenny didn't know whether she should cry or laugh. How did Georgie do it? The woman was going on seventy and couldn't see for all the diamond rings men waved in front of her!

"Yes. That's exactly what he wants to do. I can tell. I can tell from his smile and the glint in his eyes and the way he keeps patting his pocket."

"So you don't want to marry him?" Jenny tried to keep the surprise out of her voice. It seemed to her as if, so far, Georgie had married anyone who cared to ask.

"Of course I don't." Georgie's voice dropped as if it had fallen off a cliff. "I only just lost Fred. I can't marry *Klaus*. I—I never want to marry another man ever again! I want them to stop asking!"

"Georgie, you must have an idea why they keep asking," Jenny said gently. "Don't you think?"

"Well..." Georgie huffed. "Yes, I suppose I do. I know how to treat a man, you know? They're all the same. Well, not Fred. He was different. And now...and now he's dead!" She broke into hysterical sobs. "I want him back so badly!"

"Oh Georgie, you poor thing." Jenny could barely listen to the crying. How had things become so twisted for her aunt? In Jenny's memory, Georgie was still that young, vibrant woman who loved to go sailing with a friend, or hiking, with her little dog dancing around her. How had she turned into someone hiding from an unwanted marriage proposal on an ocean cruiser?

The sobs grew muffled, and then they stopped. "I'm okay," Georgie said and sniffled one last time. "I'm sorry. I'm okay. I'm fine. I'm still here."

I'm still here.

The words drilled into Jenny's heart. Yes, Georgie was still there, unlike Mom. Was that why Georgie apologized? Did she think she wasn't allowed to feel pain because she was still alive while her sister was gone?

"I know you're still here," Jenny said. "Listen, Georgie, I worry about you."

There. She'd said it. She had worried about Georgie since moving together in Nantucket. But the one time she'd told her aunt, Georgie had been so angry with Jenny she'd left the house and not come back until the next day.

Jenny had never found out where her aunt had stayed, or with whom, or what she'd been doing. But it had not been good.

"Don't worry about me. I'm fine. I'm...fine."

"All right. I believe you." Jenny didn't want her unpredictable aunt to hang up. "Listen, Aunt Georgie, have you thought any more about coming to Mendocino Cove? I would love to see you again."

"Yes, Jenny, I thought about it."

"And? Are you coming? Audrey and I would be over the moon." Jenny couldn't forget to tell Audrey to be over the moon. Hopefully, she was going to oblige.

"Yes, I'm coming." Georgie took a deep breath, like a diver before jumping into cold water. "I'm coming as soon as I can get off this boat."

"That's fantastic. Please make it happen—don't cancel it. Don't change your mind. I really want to see you. It's been too many years. And you're my only aunt." Jenny put a hand on a low, sprawling branch beside her. She needed to feel something real and warm and alive.

"No, this time I won't change my mind. You know why?"

"Because I asked you to?"

"Because Fred told me to go. He said it just before he died. *Please go back home to that cove that you came from. You have to.*" She sobbed once. "That's exactly what he said to me, Jenny."

"Okay." He'd been correct, but Jenny couldn't quite tell whether it was a nice thing to say. Georgie seemed to think so.

"He always called me his mermaid because I used to live on a beach. Isn't that so sweet? I miss him so much!"

"You were in love with Fred," Jenny said. "It's hard when a loved one dies." She knew a thing or two about that herself. "Come be with me and my daughter. We love you too."

"Your daughter doesn't even know me." Georgie sniffled.

"That's something we can fix."

"All right. I'll text you when I've booked the flight."

"Great. I'll pick you up from the airport."

"No, don't be silly. I'll take a car. It's better I be able to get around on my own, anyway."

"If you're sure." Jenny agreed. She didn't know too many women in their sixties who didn't prefer their independence.

"I'm sure." Georgie sounded like herself again. Maybe Klaus had passed by the lifeboat without detecting her, or maybe crying over Fred had brought some relief to her feelings. "By the way, darling."

"Yes?"

"I had a look at the photos you sent me of the letter saying you should have all the things in the armoire."

"Yes? What do you think?"

"I think it's very *Mom*. Rosie probably thought it was fun to see whether you would find the letters."

"Oh, I agree with that." Rosie *would* have thought it was fun—but hiding the letters under the letter *X* Jenny had stitched as a child had also been Rosie's only way of making sure it was Jenny, not Georgie, who would find what was meant for Jenny.

"Well, you go ahead and take all that stuff in the armoire like your Grandma said," Georgie said. "It's yours."

"Really?" Jenny cleared her throat. "It might be worth a lot of money, Aunt Georgie. Do you realize that?"

"Yeah, I do. Of course I do. You take it, darling. I think you need it more than me."

A wave of relief washed through Jenny. Not one of these quick, showy waves that break and get you wet in one fell swoop. No, this was one of those deliciously long, slow waves that didn't stop until they carried you off entirely, weightless and warm.

The things in the heirloom armoire were valuable. Starting with Phoebe Seabrook, who had had to run away from Nantucket, generations of women in Jenny's family had specifically collected them to accrue a nest egg in case one of the family's descendants would suddenly find themselves in need.

And Jenny had nothing.

Her adjunct salary was barely enough to pay for the car and utilities and all the little living costs she and her daughter accrued. Her position had the potential to earn more eventually. But selling a couple of the valuable heirloom antiques would help her and Audrey hold out until then.

"Thanks, Georgie," she said softly. "I really do need it. Thank you very much."

"It's yours, darling. Listen—how penniless did that man leave you?"

"Entirely penniless," Jenny admitted. "If it weren't for you letting me stay in the hotel, I don't know where I'd be."

Getting on River's nerves, probably. She pictured herself sitting on the couch in his tiny residency apartment, head hanging. Quickly, she wiped that image from her mind. It had no business there.

"Honey, I have money. You let me know if you need anything."

Jenny was touched—not too sure the offer was reliable, but it was nice of her aunt to offer. "Thank you. That's good to know."

Georgie made a strange sound. "You didn't think you could come to me, did you?"

"It's so hard to just get in touch with you," Jenny admitted. "I really appreciate that you'll let me have the heirlooms. I would like to keep a few for sentimental reasons. But a couple of the other things I want to auction off. My friend Faye knows somebody who used to work for an auction house in San Francisco. She'll take care of it for me."

Aunt Georgie cleared her throat. "Well, turn that treasure into as much gold as you can, darling. You'll need a new place to stay. I decided to finally sell the hotel."

CHAPTER 16

S he said she's going to sell the hotel?"

Aghast was the word that best described the look on her daughter's face.

Jenny picked a wild beach daisy. The headland was full of wildflowers that swayed gently in the warm breeze. Little cotton puff clouds drifted across the sky, and a formation of pelicans glided low over the sea.

"Yes, honey. That's what Georgie said. She wants to sell the hotel."

"Why? Why would she do that?" Audrey stopped and looked out at the ocean. It was blue and bright, and the waves crashed into the cliffs with joy and vigor. They obviously didn't have an aunt who planned to sell their hotel.

"We didn't get that far in the conversation." Jenny tucked the flower into her daughter's hair. It was quickly growing longer and already curled at the ends.

"Mom, I don't want flowers." Audrey sighed. "I want the hotel. I love the hotel. I'm a freakin' hotel *manager*."

"I love the hotel too. But it does belong to Georgie. I guess it holds a lot of painful memories for her. She's not able to get over them."

"That much is clear," Audrey said bitterly. The sea breeze tugged the flower askew.

Jenny smiled. "Be nice. It's her hotel, and who knows whether she doesn't need the money after all."

"It doesn't sound like there's anything I can do," Audrey said.

"My advice is to work out a business plan," Jenny said carefully. "Pitch your...your pitch, I guess. Tell her your plans and see what she has to say about it."

"You think there's hope she'll change her mind?"

"I don't know. What I do know is that there is no hope if you don't make your case."

"You're right. At least I can try." Audrey looked a little happier. She scratched her chin. "When will she come?"

Jenny's unpredictable aunt was as likely to cancel as she was to actually show up. "Who knows, Audrey? But she texted me she'll come as soon as she can. Her cruise ship will be back in a few days. She'll catch the first flight to San Jose."

"Okay. Do you think a PowerPoint presentation would scare her off?"

"I think you should cover all your bases," Jenny replied. "Make a proper presentation, have an elevator pitch, know what you'd say if we end up in front of the fireplace with a cup of cocoa in hand."

Audrey turned to her. A smile lit her eyes. "Thanks for the encouragement, Mom. Anything else you can think of that might help?"

"I feel like timing is important with your aunt. Don't talk to her about wanting to keep the hotel when she's in one of her stubborn moods. Oh, Audrey, I have no idea what I'm talking about." Jenny threw up her hands and laughed. "I haven't met my aunt in years and years. Maybe she has changed. Maybe none of this matters."

"Like you say." Audrey resumed their slow stroll over the fragrant headland. "If I don't give it a shot, I've already lost." She hooked her arm under Jenny's. "What else could I do if it doesn't work out, Mom? Can I get a job at the university, do you think?"

"You can look at the open positions, honey. They don't have a hotel school, but maybe there are staff positions you could do." Jenny would love to have her daughter work at Lizzie May. But they already lived together. Was it good for Audrey to be so close to her mother all the time? "Is there anything else you'd like to do?"

"If I can't have the old hotel, I guess I'd like to run a little B&B. That's been my plan all along. But real estate is so expensive. I would need a good salary and then save for a few years before I have enough for a down payment."

"Maybe you can find a fixer-upper," Jenny suggested. "Like Ava's old house."

"Are there any? I looked. But I don't see many houses that aren't lovingly taken care of."

"Ava's house was tucked away in a cul-de-sac, so it wasn't easily visible. It wasn't on the market, either."

"If it had been either more visible or advertised, it would have been snapped up earlier," Audrey said skeptically. "Ava got lucky."

Jenny pulled her closer and pressed a kiss on her daughter's cheek. "You can get lucky too. Ask for your own little miracle. Right now, you're basically begging the universe to ignore you. Why shouldn't you find a little house of your own?"

"Ah, optimism. It must be so nice. If only I had been born with more of it."

"It *is* nice. And it doesn't matter if you were born with it. You can always decide to be an optimist anyway."

"Right." Audrey looked amused.

"Don't *right* me, young lady." Jenny patted her daughter's hand. "You decide who you want to be. So why not be an optimist instead of a victim of circumstance? It's all in the mind, my dear. You get to choose, and you can do it right now."

"I'm sorry. You *are* right, Mom." Audrey extracted her hand from her mother's and walked close to the edge of the cliff. The breeze tugged on her hair, and her summer dress fluttered dramatically as she opened her arms wide. "Gods!" she yelled into the wind as loud as she could. "Universe! I want to work! Send me a job I'll love to do!"

Jenny laughed. "Well done, darling. That's the spirit."

Audrey dropped her arms and grinned. "Thank you very much." She pressed her hands together as if in prayer and bowed to the ocean and the sky, the waves and the horizon. "I'm much obliged for your help."

"There's Faye—and Christy." Jenny shielded her eyes with her hand. "Time to go back."

The delicate gold bracelet Jon had given her the night after her first day of teaching dangled from her wrist, and she couldn't help but wish their evening together could have been longer. Eternal, ideally. But Jon had been needed at the winery, and she'd had another lecture to prepare. It was almost time to drive over to the university again.

But Jenny had not wasted time since getting her aunt's go-ahead. She'd asked Faye to call her friend Christy, who used to work for a famous auction house and still had many friends in the business. Christy was in the area, visiting friends, and had offered to take Jenny's treasures to San Fran for her.

"Hi!" Faye sounded breathless when they met near the parking lot.

"Hi." Jenny hugged her friend and shook Christy's hand. The elderly woman was impeccably dressed in a light suit, fedora, and lipstick that matched her fingernails. "Thank you so much for coming to meet me, Christy. I have the things in my car."

"The things? My dear. They're *treasures*. I don't deal in things; I deal in treasures."

"Of course." Jenny chuckled. "Well, the treasures are all packed up in a big picnic basket. I wrapped everything up carefully."

"Ah." Christy shook her head. "That's barbaric, but hopefully also effective. Do you want me to have a look now? Here?" She wiped away a silver-white lock the wind had blown across her elegant sunglasses.

"It would be easier if you could just take them home with you," Jenny suggested. "Let me know what you think will sell and what isn't worth the trouble."

"That would be easier." Christy's mouth relaxed. "It might be a while until I get around to it. Do you mind?"

"Of course not. I'm glad you're doing it at all! Take your time."

"Good. I'll let you know when I can look through it and bring the rest back up."

"Christy is buying a house in Mendocino Cove," Faye interrupted. "Isn't that exciting?"

"That's great! Congratulations and welcome!" Jenny smiled. Christy was not only a fabulous addition to their little town but also Mrs. Agatha Simon's best friend. And Agatha needed a friend. She owned the cottage next to Billie and was prone to complaining about Billie's animals when she was bored. Christy would keep Agatha busy.

Jenny unlocked her car and handed over the loaded picnic basket. Her heart ached to see the precious items go. But her ancestors' instructions had been clear about what she was to do with the emergency collection. Sell, take the money, and run.

Or, as the case was, pay the utilities. And Jenny wanted to help Audrey buy her own car. They had a bike and a car between them, but the girl needed her independence. If Mendocino Cove was too small for Audrey to get on her feet, she would leave. And Jenny wanted her to settle here for good. If she could have, she'd have joined Audrey at the edge of the cliff, yelling into the wind, *Send my daughter someone worthy of her love! Let her settle in Mendocino Cove!*

After Faye and Christy left, Jenny turned to Audrey.

"By the way, I talked to your brother River last night."

Her daughter's eyes brightened. "Can he come? What did he say?"

Jenny smiled. She had never realized how close her kids were. They'd been a classic case of older brother and younger sister, also known as cats and dogs, when they were younger. But the events of the last two years had first united them in misery and then cemented their adult friendship.

"He can't come yet," Jenny said and got into her car. "But soon. He said he would come soon." She waited until Audrey was in the passenger seat and had closed the door. "Guess what?"

"What?"

"I think he plans on asking his girlfriend to marry him."

Audrey's eyes widened. "No! Did he say he was going to do it?"

River had prepared for a long time for the moment. He'd saved up every spare penny to buy his beloved the biggest, most beautiful diamond he could.

"He didn't give me a date. But there was something in the way he talked..." Jenny beamed. "I think he's going to ask her before he comes. In fact, I think he wants to bring her!"

"Oof." Audrey blinked. "Big news, Mom. Are you okay?"

Jenny pulled back her chin in surprise. "Why wouldn't I be okay?"

It took Audrey a beat too long to answer. "No reason. Are you happy?"

Jenny narrowed her eyes. "Why wouldn't I be okay or happy when River is getting engaged, Audrey?"

Audrey's eyes widened innocently, and she spread her hands. "No reason, Mom! I was just asking."

Jenny waited for a moment, but Audrey's eyes were as blue as they were veiled, and it was impossible to see through the curtain.

"Has he said something to you?" Jenny asked finally.

Audrey slapped her hands over her face. "Mom, will you stop? Let's go home. I'm starving. Or even better, let's go have lunch at the Mermaid Galley before you go to work. Maybe Michael made clam chowder. I'm *starving.*"

"You already said you were starving," Jenny muttered and started the car. "And if you think I haven't noticed that you didn't answer my question about your brother, you're wrong."

"I really need a car of my own," Audrey said and sighed dramatically. "I really do."

CHAPTER 17

"Y ou have been very busy lately." Gabe reached across the restaurant table and took Faye's hand. "I was afraid you were done with me."

"Um. Not quite." Faye smiled. "Though you didn't have to go through all this trouble. I could have made chicken dumplings for dinner."

"I think you must be busy enough without cooking too." His steel-blue eyes searched hers. "Either that, or you have been avoiding me."

Faye blushed and lowered her gaze. Not because she was shy, but to escape Gabe's trained eye. The man was a detective, after all, and he could spot a liar from across the room.

"I can tell I hit a nerve. Which one is it, Faye?" he asked and intertwined their fingers on the fancy tablecloth. "Busy—or avoiding me?"

Her palms were getting sweaty. No doubt he was able to tell she was nervous. How would he take the news? Baby news. Baby news. Baby... Faye coughed and pulled her hand back, pretending to need it for covering her mouth.

Without commenting, Gabe filled her glass with water from the carafe.

This was no doubt the fanciest restaurant in driving distance.

Faye took a sip. "I wonder why this place is called the Blue Heron," she said. "Why do you think that is?"

Instead of answering, Gabe leaned back in his chair. He looked impossibly sexy in his suit, which was both well-fitting and straining in all the right places.

"Faye. Up here."

She tore her gaze from his biceps. "Yes."

"What's going on?"

She shook her head. All day she had been mulling over how she should deliver the news. Bring a onesie in a gift bag and give it to him? Just blurt out she was pregnant and get it over with? Nothing seemed good.

"Okay." He picked up his wineglass and held it out. "In your own time, my love."

Faye smiled nervously and picked up her own glass. It was a pinot grigio. It was the most delicious-smelling, most fragrant and aromatic white wine she'd ever come across. She only touched her lips with the golden liquid, suppressing the urge to drink, and set down her glass like a dainty lady.

"Hmm." He tilted his head. "Do you prefer red?"

"It's delicious. It's perfect," she hastened to reassure him. He had gone to such lengths, getting them into the Blue Heron, and she was sweaty with anxiety instead of appreciative. "Lovely," she added lamely.

To her great relief, the waiter arrived with two plates that he slid artfully in front of them. "Your Caprese salad."

"Thanks," Gabe said to the waiter. "Looks good."

"You're welcome. Enjoy your meal," the waiter said and disappeared again.

"He's more talkative than you are," Gabe commented and picked up his fork.

"I'm sorry, Gabe." Faye smiled an apology. "I do love this place, and you're so sweet to take me here."

"Sweet? Sweet is the kiss of death. I'm not *sweet*," He glowered at her.

He wasn't sweet, per se. That was true. She grinned. "Forgive me. I meant to say that it's very...generous. It's very generous and extremely handsome of you to bring me here."

"That's better." He winked at her.

Faye picked up her fork. She had to tell him. She had to tell him now. She cleared her throat. "This Caprese salad looks so fresh and vibrant, don't you think? It reminds me of something else that brings, uh, freshness and vibrancy to life. Can you guess what it is?" Her lips snapped shut. It was the stupidest thing she'd ever said in her life. Faye speared a soft slice of mozzarella and stuffed it in her mouth, hoping he hadn't heard her.

"Erm." Gabe glanced at her. "What else brings more... Flowers? Or more Caprese salad?"

She swallowed. "Um, yes, I suppose they would, wouldn't they? I mean, bring freshness and...uh, *vibrancy*. To one's life, I mean. Right?"

"Yes? Is it a trick question? I can't tell."

"So good," Faye said desperately and ate a tomato with balsamic glaze.

Why couldn't she just say it? Had she watched too many videos of women making cute announcements to think straight? *I'm pregnant with your baby.* How hard was that? Not hard.

She coughed and drank water, then returned to stabbing her salad.

At least she wasn't throwing up all over the place.

They didn't talk again until the waiter returned. This time, he brought two bowls of butternut squash soup.

"Alrighty over there?" Gabe asked when they were alone again. "Did you like the vibrant salad?

"Yes." She'd already made this awkward. Maybe what she had to do now was really lean in. "Ahem. Gabe?" She picked up her spoon.

"Yes, Faye. What's up?"

She tasted her soup and then lowered her spoon and looked dead straight into his eyes. "Mm, this creamy butternut squash soup warms the soul," she said, and because it sounded so silly, she finally could genuinely smile.

"It does indeed."

"Yes. Hey—it reminds me of something that warms the heart and creates a special kind of bond. Any ideas?"

He narrowed his eyes. "Flowers again? Did you want me to bring you flowers?"

"No, I..." Faye suddenly had to laugh. She leaned back and closed her eyes and tried to get the laughter that bubbled from her belly under control. "No, my dear. It's not flowers."

He ate another spoonful of soup, but now he was smiling too. "Goodness, I thought I'd gotten you mad, not bringing flowers. I thought it'd be awkward during dinner. Do they provide vases in restaurants? I don't know."

"I'm sure they do." She smiled at him. "Next time, absolutely do bring me flowers. I like peonies."

They finished the soup, and then the waiter reappeared to take the bowls and deliver the main course.

Faye took a tiny taste. "Ahem," she said delicately.

Gabe put his fork down. The look in his eyes was slightly pained. "Okay. Go ahead with your weird little riddle."

"Thank you." Faye cleared her throat. "This perfectly grilled salmon with tangy lemon butter sauce is absolutely divine. Gabe, did you know salmon like to travel upstream? It reminds me of another journey that requires total dedication. Can you guess what it might be?"

He frowned. "A journey. A dedicated journey. What sort of journey?"

"A journey of...self-development." Faye popped a morsel of buttery-soft salmon in her mouth and felt her eyes widen. "It just melts in your mouth! How delicious."

"Can I eat while I think?" He picked up his fork and speared a piece of fish. "It really is good. Do you want to travel? That sort of journey?" He glanced at her. "We could do a short trip if you like. Dad is doing well. I can hire someone to check in with him."

"Oh. No, I don't want to travel. But thank you." Her heart sank a little. "Do *you* want to travel?" A kid would make traveling hard. At least for a while. Twenty years or so, according to Billie.

"Not particularly. There isn't exactly anywhere to go where it's nicer than here." He had a sip of his wine. "I only offered because of your dedicated journey there. Oh—do you want to travel on your own? Do you have an eye on a yoga camp or whatever it's called?"

"They're called retreats, I think," Faye said and ate the last perfectly roasted potato. "And no, I haven't got any retreats planned."

"Workshops?"

"No workshops either."

He lowered his head. "Classes?"

"Hmm." She rolled the stem of her wine glass between her fingers. "Yes, maybe a class." Lamaze classes to control the unbearable pain of childbirth. Though Billie had said it wasn't that bad. Both her boys had popped out quickly and elegantly, so maybe there was hope.

"A class. Got it."

"Would you like dessert?" the waiter asked and stacked the plates on his arm.

"Faye?"

"Molten chocolate cake, please."

"I'll have an espresso," Gabe added, and the waiter disappeared. A short minute later, he returned with the plumpest little cake Faye could wish for.

Either she was sick and everything made her nauseated, or she was not sick and everything tasted delicious.

"Come to mama," she said happily. When she realized what she'd just said, she almost dropped her cake fork. Her gaze flew to Gabe.

He was grinning, one hand on his espresso cup. "All right, I'm ready," he said. "Last course, last riddle. Go ahead, Miss McAllister."

Faye's cheeks had flushed warm. "Okay. Um... How about this?" Again, laughter bubbled up. Then she leaned forward, closed her eyes seductively, and made her voice velvety smooth. "And now, the grand finale! This molten chocolate lava cake is simply irresistible. It symbolizes something that will blow our minds and fill our lives with sweetness. Any guesses?"

Gabe leaned forward too so that his face was only inches from hers. He trailed a finger along her jawline. "I don't know—mama. Why don't you just come out and tell me?"

His touch made Faye's breathing quicken. "I'm pregnant with your baby, Gabe," she whispered.

His smile jumped from his lips to his eyes, and he cradled her face with his hand. "I love you, Faye. Thank you for finally telling me. I thought I was going crazy waiting for you to make up your mind."

The look between them said everything she needed to know.

"I love you too, Gabe," she whispered.

"Are you done eating? Let's go home."

She looked from her lover—no, the love of her life—to the molten chocolate cake on her plate. Rising out of her seat, she kissed him on the lips. Then she sank back in her chair with an apologetic look and picked up her fork. "I'm almost done, my love."

CHAPTER 18

Ava picked up a small branch of dry driftwood and tossed it into the blazing bonfire. The flames merrily embraced it. Watching it burn, she took a tentative sip of her watermelon agua fresca. It was good. Fresh watermelon juice with a splash of lime juice and a touch of syrup for sweetness, served with mint leaves over ice. She sat back and let her gaze wander over the beautiful beach. The sun was about to set, casting both sky and water into fiery gold and throwing long shadows.

"Hey, Ava." Jenny joined her, sitting beside her on the dry, sun-bleached log. "Pretty nice, isn't it?"

"It's breathtaking. I can't believe we get to experience this." Ava cheered with her watermelon drink, and Jenny cheered back with a virgin piña colada.

In honor of Faye's pregnancy, all drinks of the night were alcohol-free. The foods were things like teddy-bear-shaped sandwiches with fillings like ham and cheese, turkey and cranberry sauce, or cucumber and cream cheese, and cut fruit on skewers, made to look like baby rattles.

"She looks radiant," Ava noted and looked at Faye. Faye was standing across the fire, tucked under Gabe's arm, her arms slung around his waist, laughing at something Jon was saying.

"I'm so happy for her." Jenny bit off the head of her teddy bear sandwich and grinned. "She's going to be the best mom. But boy, is she in for a ride."

"I find myself staring a little too long at baby pictures when I come across them," Ava said and smiled. "But goodness, I can't imagine going through all that again."

"Aha. You are growing into your grandma shoes." Jenny licked a spot of cranberry sauce off her finger. "You have a daughter, don't you?"

"I do. Her name is Zoe. She's going to turn twenty-four in August."

"Similar age to Audrey, then. What does Zoe do?"

"She has a small online business selling custom-order cupcakes. She just moved in with her boyfriend, Timothy. He's ten years older than her, and he has an apartment in Seattle."

"Ten years? That's a big age gap. You don't sound very happy about it."

"I'm not sure he's right for her." Ava sighed. "I don't have anything specific against him; he's nice enough. But he's got big energy. He seems to have absorbed her like a star absorbs a moon."

"Meanwhile, my girl doesn't seem to have any interest in dating at all." Thoughtfully, Jenny ate the rest of her sandwich and tossed her paper napkin into the crackling fire. "Does Zoe share her feelings with you?"

"To be honest, we haven't spent much time together since she started dating Timothy. She doesn't even know that I'm in Mendocino Cove." Let alone that Ava wasn't going to come back to Seattle. That was a conversation still to be had—if and when Zoe had a moment to spare from the latest Timo-drama.

A clinking sound rang out over the beach like a crystal bell.

Billie stood barefoot in the sand, holding up her glass and tapping a silver spoon against it. The last rays of the sinking sun made her brown hair glow like liquid bronze, and her smiling face was illuminated by the crackling bonfire. "Here's a virgin toast to Faye. Faye, darling, you are the kind of girlfriend everyone wants and we're lucky enough to have. We are so proud to know you." She stopped and swallowed.

"Aww, poor Bills is going to cry." Jenny put a hand to her heart.

Ava smiled. She wanted to be a best friend again too. The three women, Billie, Jenny, and Faye, were so close. Ava knew she was not back in the circle yet, but once they had all been inseparable. If she moved here, she could revive their old friendship.

And her friends in Seattle... Ava would do whatever she could to keep them close. They'd been there for her when she had been at her loneliest. Seattle wasn't that far away, and maybe she could talk her girls there into visiting Mendocino Cove sometime.

"So, anyway." Billie cleared her throat. "I just wanted to say, Faye, that I'll be there when you need a babysitter to catch a nap."

"Hear, hear," Gabe said and cheered Billie back with his sparkling blueberry limeade.

"Thank you, Billie." Clearly, Faye was also touched to tears.

"And I'll be there when you're too tired to cook. Let me know, and I'll bring you two foods fresh from the grill at the winery," Jon said and raised his glass.

"Thanks, man," Gabe said and pulled Faye closer.

"I'll chip in with laundry and ironing. The hotel has the professional capabilities to clean all two hundred sorts of spit-up from bibs and onesies." Jenny also raised her glass.

Audrey followed her mother's example. "I'll pamper your guests at the hotel, so you don't have to," she declared cheerfully.

Ava didn't know what was left to offer. But she wanted to give Faye something too. "I'll take care of your garden and shop," she declared and raised her glass. "I'll buy you onesies with stupid sayings on them and too many tiny snap buttons, and I'll look the other way when you don't use them." She winked at Faye.

"Thank you. You are also the best...the best..." Faye choked up.

Gabe laughed and pulled her closer, then raised his glass. "In the name of my lovely partner and mother of my unborn son, thank you all. You truly are the best friends anyone could have. Cheers!"

"Unborn daughter," Faye corrected him happily. "You guys are the best. Cheers."

"Cheers!" they echoed and sipped their drinks. Then Jon picked up his guitar and Audrey her ukulele, and soon, their sweet, cheerful music drifted over the beach. The sun set, and the moon rose like a mysterious golden coin in the velvety night sky.

A little later, Lex, his brother, Michael and Hannah from the Mermaid Galley, and Agatha and her friends Christy and Barbara joined them on the beach. They brought trays full of lobsters and shrimps, lemon-ricotta linguine and truffle mac and cheese, roast barbecue ribs and steak and pulled pork, cupcakes, and colorful bags stuffed with baby gifts.

Ava helped set everything up and congratulated Faye and Gabe, then sat on one of the driftwood logs to eat a dinner of pulled pork sliders with pineapple coleslaw.

Everyone was in such a happy, radiant mood. In a perverse, backfiring sort of way, their closeness made her feel lonely. It was a subtle effect, but it was starting to drain her.

She wiped her fingers and stood to throw her paper napkin and plate into the fire. What was her husband doing right now? Having dinner with Ginny at the country club?

"Do you want to walk down to the water?" Jenny asked and hooked her arm under Ava's.

Ava threw her a grateful look. "I'd love to, Jenny."

The farther they walked away from the fire, the cooler the night became. Ava was glad she'd brought the long alpaca cardigan to cover her thin shirt dress. The water was cold but refreshing when she stepped into it.

A sea lion raised her head and barked at them. By her side was a black pup who slept cuddled up to her mom.

"How cute," Ava said and stopped to admire the pretty pair. "I think the evening's theme is making me miss my daughter."

"That's Polly," Jenny said. "It's okay to pass close by. We won't disturb her. Hi, baby." She kept walking, and Ava hurried to keep up.

They were right between the sea lion mom and the ocean. Cutting off a mom's escape route was never a good idea, but tonight, on this beach, everyone seemed to be best friends.

As if agreeing with Ava's thoughts, Polly barked one more time and then let her head fall back onto the sand with a satisfied grunt.

They strolled along the waterline in the silvery moon light. Jenny started talking about the lecture she was going to give the next morning, and Ava, genuinely interested in both the topic and her friend's feelings, kept asking questions.

"Jen-ny! A-va!"

They turned. The friends were scattered around the fire, talking and laughing, but Billie was waving with both arms for them to come back.

"Maybe it's time for musical chairs, or Agatha wants us to eat more cupcakes," Jenny said.

Ava nodded. "We'd better go back and see what she wants."

CHAPTER 19

"I'm glad you didn't get lost in the night," Billie said when Ava and Jenny finally arrived. "It's impossible to see anyone beyond the fire circle. Ava, you have a visitor."

Ava raised an eyebrow. "A *visitor*?"

"Yes. It's Bruno," Billie said and exhaled. "Girl, I didn't know what to do. He heard us on the beach and came walking up to me, cool as a cucumber. I brought him inside and gave him a drink—I think he just arrived in Mendocino Cove. Jon said we'd have to check in with you before he could stay. Do you want to see him?"

"Yes. Yes, of course I'll see him." Confusion made Ava shaky. She tucked her hands in the pockets of her cardigan. "Is he in the living room?"

"Yes. Go ahead. We're out here if you need us."

"Thanks." Ava turned and hurried, as fast as one could hurry walking barefoot in sand, to meet her husband. On the patio, she wiped her feet, pulled open the sliding door, and stepped inside.

"Bruno?"

Empty. The comfortable couches in front of the fireplace were empty. So were the armchairs in the reading corner and the wicker chairs by the windows. She took a shaky breath.

"Ava."

She turned around. There was her husband, standing in the door that led to the lobby. "Bruno!"

"I thought you weren't coming."

"I'm here. For a moment, *I* thought you had left again."

"I just went to wash my hands." Bruno pointed over his shoulder. He had lost weight. It suited him, and it made him look younger. Almost like he looked when they first got married.

He smiled and opened his hands. "I know. I'm wasting away. The doctor said it was good for me, so I don't mind."

"You look good." She smiled back tentatively.

For a moment, they just looked at each other.

"Why are you here?" Ava asked finally.

"I came to talk," he said quietly. "Can we please talk?"

"Can we talk?" Ava tilted her head. "In all these years, you never came to talk. You never cared to talk."

"That's not true." He lowered his gaze. "I tried. But it was never enough."

Ava sighed. Here they went again. The excuses, the wanting too much from him, the averted gaze. "Bruno," she said. "Don't make it my problem. It *wasn't* enough. We completely lost touch with each other. There's no longer a real connection, only housekeeping matters and that eternal, terrible dance of me trying to get more and you trying to give less. I won't do it any longer. I'm done. I love you, but I'm done."

"I want more connection too, Ava," he said quietly. "But I didn't know what I had to do. I was failing at being a husband. I wasn't failing at working; nothing made me feel ashamed in the office. So that's where I spent my time."

"I know. I know. But you abandoned me. I didn't have an office and adoring secretaries to make me feel good about myself—"

"Ginny doesn't adore me," Bruno said patiently. "I don't know if she even likes me. She never volunteered that information, and I never asked because I don't care if she does. I pay her well, and she's a competent secretary. That's the sum total of our relationship. I promise."

Ava couldn't help but feel relief. He had said it before, but this time, he explained. She cleared her throat. "You interrupted me. I was saying that it was easy for you to go to work and forget about me. I didn't have the option." She sat on an armchair. "The thing is, Bruno...even if I had had the option to spend most of my time with other people and in other places than our home, I wouldn't have taken it. I cared too much about you."

Bruno sighed and went to glance out of the window. "You know what Ginny said when she dropped me off at the airport?"

Ava shut her eyes. "What?"

"She said that women most dread being abandoned, and men fear humiliation," he said. "We each do whatever we must to protect ourselves."

Ava looked up. "It's true for me."

"It's true for me too."

She smiled sadly. "So if I come to you because you work too much, and I feel lonely—"

He turned to her. "Then I feel ashamed because I didn't make you happy. I bury myself in even more work because I can't bear the shame, and—"

"And I feel even more abandoned."

"And I work even more."

She looked at her hands. "Then men and women are incompatible. It sounds like we're done."

"No." He sat beside her. "No, we're not done, Ava. We'll never be done because I love you."

"I love you too," she said. "But it doesn't matter. A few insights don't change things. I can't be lonely because you feel bad around me."

He exhaled a tense breath. "Can we try?"

"Bruno." She wanted to take his hand. But it would send the wrong signal and make things harder. "I tried too long and too hard. I'm done trying."

"Can *I* try?" Now he took her hands. "Please let me try. I didn't understand how lonely you were, Ava. I only saw how it made me feel like a failure."

She shook her head. "What are you going to do?"

"I don't know. Whatever it takes to make you feel loved."

Ava couldn't help but smile. "Listen to you. What about your golf and your work?"

"I'm going to give them up. Well, mostly."

"Aha." She pulled her hands from his.

"I mean it. I already arranged it with the junior partners of the company. They will step up and fill my shoes. I'll make myself available to consult with them once a week for the next half year, and after that, they'll have me once a month. In a year, I'll be fully out. All done. No more. It's already settled."

"I don't know what to do with this." Ava stood. "It sounds too good to be true, Bruno."

He stood too. "Can I take you out to breakfast tomorrow morning?"

"Where are you staying?" Ava asked.

"I found a motel in Fern Beach. It's only half an hour's drive from Mendocino Cove."

"Then let's have breakfast tomorrow morning."

She looked at him. He had come to talk; he had rearranged his schedule to leave the company. He wanted to have breakfast together... Could people change? Was it possible?

"I'll pick you up," he said.

She tilted her head. "Nine o'clock?"

"Nine o'clock," he promised. "I'm looking forward to it."

"Are you really?"

"Yes, really. I've always enjoyed breakfast with you."

"You were reading your newspaper, not having breakfast with me."

He took her hands into his and kissed first one, then the other. "I drifted away from the person I want to be with because it was the easy thing to do."

She pulled her hands away. "You should probably leave now. I'd like to go back to my friends."

He turned to go. "I'll see you tomorrow morning," he said. "Goodnight, Ava."

"Goodnight."

He left, and the door swung shut.

It was the first time in a long time they had bid each other good night. It was the first time in an even longer time he had opened up.

Ava knew she loved him. What she didn't know was whether she had enough hope to give him a second chance.

But she could eat breakfast with him.

"Please don't let me down," she whispered.

CHAPTER 20

"You look nice. Turn around." Billie, coffee cup in hand, leaned against the kitchen island.

"No, I'm not turning around. That's silly." Ava felt warmth crawl up her neck as if she were a blushing bride. She had donned her favorite white cotton dress—knee-length, simple A-line, with pretty lace hems—and the simple gold armbands from Italy she liked so much.

"You're *pretty*," Billie said and smiled. "You haven't changed much at all since you were a teen. Or maybe it's the fact that your hubby came chasing after you?"

Ava exhaled. "I don't even know if he's going to show up today or if a golf course along the way is going to distract him." She crossed her arms and hugged herself.

"Well, you're still pretty," Billie insisted. "What do you want? Do you want him to show up here and sweep you away? Do you have the energy for another round of testing your marriage? Or are you simply over it?"

"I don't know." Ava shrugged her shoulders helplessly. "I thought I was done. I really did. But when he showed up the night before and said he is getting out of the company... I don't know anymore."

"You have two options," Billie said fondly. "Either go with it or don't. I wouldn't waste time in the murky middle."

"But Billie, most of life happens in the murky middle." Ava smiled back. "And since I don't know what I want anymore, that's *exactly* where I'll have to settle for now. I'll go with the flow and see how things turn out."

"Alrighty then." Billie's eyes softened. "You have more patience than I do. That's for sure. Hey—" She put a hand to her ear. "I hear a car."

Bruno had arrived. Ava felt her heartbeat quicken. "Is it him?"

"I don't know, Ava." Billie grinned. "You sound like a teenager with a crush. Are you sure you are in the murky middle?"

"I am so. Believe me."

The doorbell rang, and Billie went to answer it. Moments later, she returned with Bruno in tow. In his hands, he held the most enormous bouquet of roses.

"Good morning, Ava," he said and handed her the flowers.

"Good morning. Uh—thank you, Bruno. These are fantastic." She didn't need to bring the flowers up to her face. Already, their sweet scent filled the kitchen.

"I'll go get a vase," Billie announced and left, even though the vases were in the kitchen island cabinet.

Carefully, she laid the roses on the kitchen island. "Bruno, what's gotten into you? How long do you think you can keep this up?" she asked gently.

He smiled. "It took a wake-up call, but when it came, I knew what I had to do. I want to make up for what I missed and what I messed up. Instead of work and golf, you are my priority from now on."

"How terrifying," Ava said and smiled back.

"I am the one who is terrified. I'm terrified of losing you."

"I didn't know whether you would even notice I was gone."

"It took me a moment before I understood what was happening," he admitted. "I was literally waking up to the reality of losing you."

"But I don't want you to twist yourself into someone you're not, Bruno," Ava insisted. "I don't want to play games. I want what's real."

"I want what's real too," he said quietly. "I'm starting a new page, doing what actually matters to me. And growing old working and playing golf—well, that's not the reality I want. I know it's how I acted, but that's all over now."

"What *do* you want? I'm genuinely curious."

"I want a cup of coffee," he said. "And I want to spend my life with you. I want to travel. I really want to take a trip to Italy together. Eat pasta in Roman street cafés and listen to the opera in Verona and take walks in Tuscany."

It sure sounded nice.

Ava went to pour a morning cup for her husband. "At least one of those wishes is easy to fulfill." She handed him the mug.

"Thank you," he said sincerely and drank. "Oh, that's good. Did you make it?"

"No, Billie did. She's a wizard in the kitchen."

"I am that." Billie was coming back into the kitchen, a big vase in her hands, and went to fill it at the sink. "You know, if you guys want to have breakfast on the dock, you are most welcome," she said casually. "Lex and I were out there earlier, but he already ate at home and hardly touched anything. You'll have the place to yourself too. I have to run over to Lizzie May for a meeting with my wildlife biologists." She turned off the faucet and dried her hands.

"I don't want to impose," Bruno said hesitatingly. "Ava? What would you like to do?"

"Let me show you the dock," Ava said. With this offer on the table, she suddenly no longer wanted to go to some restaurant that wasn't half as good as Billie's breakfast, nor half as pretty as her dock. "The view alone is worth the trip."

"Whatever you decide is fine with me. I'll get going." Billie handed Ava the vase. "Maybe I'll see you for dinner."

"Thanks, Billie. Bye." Ava arranged the roses in the vase.

"I forgot to mention that there are warm Eccles cakes in the oven," Billie said over her shoulder from the door. She waved, and then she left.

"Thank you, Billie!" Bruno called after her. Then he looked at Ava. "She seems very nice."

"Yes, she is. Billie was my best friend when I lived here. She still is one of my best friends."

"What about your friends in Seattle? Have you told them you are staying here?"

"Not yet," Ava admitted. "They know I was thinking about visiting here, but I haven't talked to them since before I left. They're all busy with their own lives right now. Soon I'll have to get in touch and confess I'm buying a house. They're not going to be too happy." No, they wouldn't take kindly to Ava jumping ship. She'd have to present it as an opportunity to visit her in California. Mendocino Cove had a lot more sun than Seattle and a lot less rain; maybe that would tempt them.

"Then come back with me," Bruno said softly.

Ava shook her head. "That part of my life is over, Bruno." She had sat long enough in the house on the hill, lonely and alone and fed up with marble tiles and white on white. She wanted color, and beach bonfires with good friends, and rich foods that tasted like joy. Even if her pants were starting to get a little tight and she wasn't the same size she'd been as a teen at all anymore. "I want to live in my house here in Mendocino County." She cleared her throat. "Whatever we two decide, that's one thing I already know."

To her surprise, Bruno smiled. "We'll take that into consideration yet."

She looked up. "We will?" Bruno would consider moving here, just to be with her?

He nodded. "You came to Seattle for me. It should be your turn to decide where we live now. We can still travel to Italy. And Portugal. I really want to see the sea in Portugal."

"Yes," she said softly. "That would still be possible."

He touched a rose. "Ava, what's an Eccles cake? I've never heard that before in my life."

Ava laughed. "I didn't know either, but Billie makes them often. They're named after the town of Eccles in England." She opened the oven, slipped on a mitten, and pulled out the baking sheet. "Here." She handed one of the sweet, round pastries to Bruno. Similar to a small tart, it looked rustic and charming, with the concentric swirls on the slightly domed, golden brown top giving it a unique look.

He bit into it. "Hmm. Good. What's that—currants?"

"Yes." Ava hadn't had breakfast yet and took one too. She bit into the flaky puff pastry. "Mmm, it is good, isn't it? I can taste cinnamon and nutmeg." Baked to perfection, the currants had become tender, and the sugar caramelized.

She glanced at her husband. Who would have thought two weeks ago that they would taste pastries together in a sun-flooded kitchen in a cottage at the sea?

"Goodness, they are delicious. Perfect for a cup of coffee or tea. Slightly sticky too." Bruno went to wash his fingers in the sink and looked out the window. "Is that the dock Billie mentioned? Dear me, what a beautiful property."

Ava joined him, letting the warm water run over her hands as she looked outside. "Yes, that's it. Looks like something out of a stylish magazine, doesn't it?"

He nodded. "It makes me want to see your house," he said suddenly. "Your childhood home? Is it as pretty as this one?"

She smiled. He had never been to Mendocino Cove—they'd come close, but it had never seemed worth the hassle of driving over the mountain range. "My house is also pretty," she confirmed. "Of course it's different. These are the only cottages in the area. My parents had an arts and crafts house. Our property also goes to the water, but it sits on a bluff. You have to climb down to the beach." She should have had a peep at the beach when she was there. "I'm afraid the wooden staircase might be in bad shape."

"Does it have a garden?" He was still looking out of the window.

"It has a beautiful garden. Also not in the best shape, but I loved it so much as a kid."

"Why did you never garden in Seattle?" Bruno turned to look at her.

She shrugged. "I was so busy. I had some attempts at container gardening, remember? I bought all those terracotta pots with such high hopes. But it wasn't like here."

"Too gray?"

Ava hummed agreement as she watched the flowers sway in Billie's garden. "And the temperatures are milder in Mendocino Cove too. Let's have breakfast here," she suggested. "We won't find a more beautiful setting or better tasting pastries."

He grinned. "I was hoping you would say that. I love the idea of sitting on that dock and having nothing to do but enjoy myself for once."

They put a few more Eccles cakes into a breadbasket, filled the thermos with coffee, and went to sit on the dock. The breakfast table was still set and full of Billie's usual breakfast goodies. The sun had kept the eggs and almond croissants warm, and they ate and talked about Zoe and watched the cormorants and pelicans dive into the water.

But then Bruno fell quiet.

"Are you all right?" Ava asked finally. "What are you thinking about?"

He turned to her. "Tell me about your childhood home?"

She braced herself. "I'm buying it, Bruno. It's already happening."

"You said it was neglected."

"Yes." Maybe it was his silence or the sudden change of topic, but Ava felt guilty and defensive for not having included Bruno in the decision. But what her husband said next, she couldn't have predicted.

"Let me fix it up," he said. "I used to be pretty good with tools."

"Oh." She blinked in surprise. "I'm afraid it's a bit past the point of cosmetic problems. The ceiling inside has caved in, and there are some structural issues that need to be addressed."

Bruno nodded. "I see."

"I can show you, if you want," she said hesitatingly. "I didn't mean to make you feel bad—again."

He smiled and shook his head. "A collapsed ceiling isn't the same as an unhappy wife, Ava. I'm smart enough to see the difference."

"So, do you want to see my house?" she asked.

"Of course I want to see your house." He sounded surprised.

A wave of relief washed through her. "Good! We could go right now, if you want."

"I do want." But he didn't move. He was staring out at the ocean. Then he frowned. "I'm sorry we never came out here, my dear. I don't know why we didn't."

Ava knew why, but she didn't say it. It had never been worth the trouble to him. There'd always been some sort of timeline to get up or down the coast, and never a free day to stray across the mountains for nostalgia's sake.

"Ava, let me fix it for you," he said.

"I told you—"

"I know. I know. I'm not going to try to do the roof by myself. But let me take care of it for you. I'm an architect, after all."

"Hmm. I don't know. I know how it used to be. I'd like it to be like that again, mostly."

"Your skills, my vision? We'll do it together?" He put his open hand on the table, and after a moment, Ava put her hand into his. His eyes lit up, and his fingers closed tenderly. "You tell me what you want, and I'll take care of it. Let me start making it up to you."

"For real?"

"Yes. Let me build my wife the house of her dreams."

Slowly, she nodded. "Okay. If you're sure. It will take a while. You'd have to stay here."

"I don't have anything to go back to," he said. "I arranged for weekly zoom meetings with the junior partners."

"What about golf? What about...Ginny?"

"I'm not about to golf away my second chance with you," he said. "And what about Ginny? Do you still not believe me?"

"I do," she said hastily. "I do believe you."

"She still works for the company," Bruno said after a moment of silence. "She doesn't lose her job just because I'm gone. Are you worried about that?"

She pulled her hand away and stood. "Come on," she said. "Let's drive over to the house. I think it's no longer trespassing when we enter the property—it's almost mine already, and the seller doesn't care one bit. I swear he completely forgot the house was part of his real estate portfolio."

CHAPTER 21

Ava closed her car door and clasped her hands, watching her husband closely. As an architect, Bruno was discerning when it came to houses. It would be a relief to know he liked hers. "This is it," she said.

The corners of Bruno's mouth dropped with respect. "Whoa. I didn't expect something this beautiful."

Ava exhaled. "You really mean it?"

"Of course I mean it. It's in rough shape, but it's a beauty." He smiled. "Don't worry. We can fix this, Ava."

She glanced at him, feeling a faint blush creep up her cheeks. *We. We can fix this.* He really wanted to make this work. "Let's go have a closer look."

Side by side, they walked onto the property. "The flowers used to be my mother's pride and joy." Ava pointed at the leftovers of beds and pots. "I don't think the seller ever came here. Isn't that the weirdest thing?"

"Real estate was cheap when your parents sold this house," Bruno said. "Buying oceanfront property was a popular investment opportunity back then. But not everyone knows how to manage their investments. If the buyer was a Silicon Valley millionaire who had newly come into money but didn't yet know how to manage it—I'm not surprised some things slipped their minds. Or their portfolios."

"I think it's a shame," Ava said. "But I'm biased. I loved this house. I loved living here."

"I didn't realize how much you missed it."

"I didn't realize myself, or I would have come back long ago. Maybe I wouldn't have felt so lonely and dependent." Ava picked a wild poppy.

The sea breeze had blown away the delicate orange petals, and the heavy, ridged seed capsule sprinkled poppy seeds into her palm. She blew them into the wild garden.

"Maybe. Your parents died too young. You should have had them too," Bruno said and squinted up at the building, taking a few steps to the side to see better. "I see what you're saying about the roof. Erm. Ava?"

"What?"

"Please tell me you didn't go inside."

"Uh. Maybe just a little."

He blanched under his tan. "Are you—don't do stuff like that, Ava. It scares me. Can't you see how dangerous it is?" He ran a hand through his hair. "What if the roof had collapsed on you? The floors must be rotten too."

"I was careful." She smiled. "Maybe that's one thing the long drought was good for—everything seems dry. At least I didn't see any rot inside." She showed him the key she'd recovered last time. "Do you want to have a look? We can stand in the door."

He looked torn. "How far did you go inside? Tell the truth."

"I went everywhere," she confessed. "Even upstairs."

He muttered something under his breath, but Ava climbed the stairs to the front porch and unlocked the door. "Look," she said and stepped back.

Bruno joined her. "Beautiful," he murmured. "It feels peaceful despite the damage."

"Do you like it?" She couldn't get enough of him saying it.

"I do. But we're not going inside. I want nothing falling on us. It's a pretty stupid way to go after all the kale smoothies you made."

"You never drank a single one," she mentioned, surprised he even remembered.

"They're terrible." He grinned at her. "But at least you are healthy. I'm not about to let a rotten beam change that."

"I want to show you the backyard." Ava would have liked to take Bruno's hand, but she couldn't quite get herself to reach out. What if, in another week, his yearning for a good game of golf or another work project overcame him again? She had to guard her heart. Yo-yo love felt even worse than yo-yo dieting.

"Here's a path," she said instead and led the way around the house.

"Look at the sea," he exclaimed when he rounded the old rhododendron and saw the view from the bluff. "I know at least twenty people who'd buy this place sight unseen."

She frowned. "I'm not selling it, Bruno."

He turned, and when he saw her face, he laughed. "I was just saying it's truly a beautiful property, Ava. Of course you won't sell this. It's lucky you could get it back." He paused. "Sorry. I don't have a say in this, do I?"

She smiled. "It depends on what it is you're saying, Bruno. You can tell me how much you like it. I'll listen to that all day long. You *can't* say you want to sell it for profit. If you do, I'll ask you to leave and take that negative karma off my pretty property."

"Got it." He chuckled. "I like a woman who knows what she wants."

"What I want right now is to fix this thing." She looked at the roof, squinting into the hazy air. Clouds were quickly invading the azure sky of the morning. "Are you sure you want to take this on? It's a lot of work, and it'll take time."

He joined her in squinting at the roof. "Of course. That's what I do, Ava. Designing houses, building them, and fixing old ones. It's my jam."

"It's my jam?" she echoed him. "Really? Who says that anymore?"

"I do." He wiped his cheek. "Hey. Is it raining?"

A drop landed on her forehead. "Is it?"

"I thought you just said the lack of rain was a problem!" Bruno wiped another drop away.

"It is! The drought forces people to ration water and keeps the tourists away. It's a huge problem."

"Well, then Mendocino Cove is in luck." He laughed.

"It is. Look at that." Ava turned to look out at the ocean, wiping away a few strands of hair the stiffening breeze blew into her face.

Sweeping in like a heavy velvet curtain on a theater stage, leaden clouds entered the scene. One after the other, they crowded the sky and muted the brilliant sunlight.

Another raindrop fell on Ava, and another, faster and faster until the clouds merged into a solid blanket above them, and the gates opened for good. Rain gushed down as if the clouds were buckets tipping out the water the good people of Mendocino Cove had so carefully saved up.

"Eek! Oh no!" Ava looked down at herself, laughed, and crossed her arms over her chest. Her thin, light dress was not meant to get wet! "Should we leave?"

"Too late now." Bruno raked his hair out of his forehead and smiled. "We're already soaked."

"Let's see whether we can get into the shed," Ava said and waved for him to follow her.

Dripping wet, she weaved her way past overgrown bushes and flower beds, remembering the winding stone paths crisscrossing the garden. Finally, there was her shed in the farthest corner of the garden, as close to the sea as possible.

The shed was where they'd kept the gardening tools and potting supplies. It had a big bay window on account of the ocean view and a large window seat filling the bay nook. It had been Ava's spot to read books and her favorite place to watch a rainstorm.

"What's this?" Bruno came to a stop close behind her, finding refuge from the streaming rain under the narrow eave of the gabled roof.

"Our gardening shed." Ava tugged the vines from the door. The heat of her husband's body radiated through her thin, wet dress, warming her. "Feel the ledge over the door for the key? Maybe it's still there."

Bruno did and found the key in another small glass jar. It took a few tries, but he managed to get it out and unlock the door. He peeked inside. "Looks safe enough." He stood aside, holding the door for her.

Ava slipped past him into her beloved hideaway. It looked exactly as she had left it, minus the potted plants that used to brighten the inside. But the large terracotta planters with their reliefs of garlands of leaves and grapes still stood in the back, and the wooden shelves still smelled like earthy soil and soft moss. Faded vintage botanical prints showing intricate illustrations of flowers and plants hung on the walls. In the dim light, Ava went to the bay window and sank onto the soft window seat. One pane had a small crack, but otherwise, it was intact.

She heard the door close but didn't turn to look. The wild spectacle of the storm outside mesmerized her. The rain drummed against the window and the tin roof, pitting the soil and the sea, washing the dust off leaves and trees and flowers.

After a moment, Bruno sat beside her. "Ava," he said under his breath. "You are beautiful."

"Oh." She glanced down. She'd forgotten about her clinging dress. Her underwear was plainly visible under the soaked fabric. There was nothing lying around she could grab to cover up, either. The blankets that used to be here had moved with the family to Seattle. Ava pulled on her dress, unsuccessfully trying to unstick the wet cotton from her skin.

"No—don't do that, love. Let me see you." Bruno brushed his fingertips over her cheeks, and she leaned into the warmth of his touch. "Can I kiss you, Ava?" he murmured. "I won't if you say no. But I want to. I want you."

"Yes," she whispered. "Kiss me, Bruno."

Her husband leaned in, and their lips met in a tender kiss. His lips were gentle, but the longer they kissed, the more they demanded.

She closed her eyes. "Bruno," she whispered, her mouth moving against his. "This is wrong."

"I don't know anything that's more right," he murmured. "You taste like rain and feel like silk. And I love you."

"I love you too." Ava melted against him as he ran his hands through her hair and down her back, his touch sending sparks of warmth throughout her body. He kissed her neck, trailing down to her collarbone before moving back up to capture her lips. She trembled as he cupped one of her hands, interlocking their fingers together, guiding her arm around his neck until she, too, was hugging him. The intensity of their embrace increased until neither one could hold back any longer;

they needed each other in that moment like air to breathe.

Ava let out a sigh of relief as her back hit the soft pillow of the window nook. She was lost in the feeling of his lips on hers, his hands on her body, and the way he made her feel alive.

"Are you sure?" he murmured, pulling away too far and too long to see her face. "I'm sure," she replied, hugging him back to her. They moved together in a rhythm that was both familiar and new, two souls intertwined in the most intimate expression of love.

Afterward, they stayed in each other's arms for what seemed like an eternity while they watched the rain wash away the last of the summer dust. It was a radiant renewal, a fresh beginning.

Finally, Ava straightened so her lips reached her husband's ear. "What we just did—it means nothing," she whispered.

He turned his head so he could look into her eyes. "It means everything," he murmured. "To me, it means everything."

The look in his dark eyes made her heart flutter as much as his touch had done. "How did you change so much in such a brief time? Is it real?" She ran a hand through his moussed-up hair, smoothing it back.

"I didn't change," Bruno said in a low, serious voice. "I just forgot. Why I was working so much. How and who I want to be. It didn't feel right, like slowly wandering down the wrong path. My insides knotted up tighter and tighter until I was wound so tight I couldn't hear you anymore." He exhaled. "But when you said you were done... That came through loud and clear. It was my wake-up call."

"It surprised me. I didn't think you'd notice so quickly."

"Oh, I noticed." He propped himself on an arm and kissed the spot between her collarbones. "I turned and ran. I ran as fast as I could to catch up with you."

Ava smiled and extracted herself gently from his embrace. Her careful plans of keeping him at arm's length had unraveled enough for the day. "The rain has stopped, Bruno. The clouds are gone. It's sunny. We should go back before people wonder where we are."

"Let's move here together," he murmured and crossed his hands behind his head. "We'll go to the beach and read books and make love. In the evenings, we'll sit outside and drink wine."

"Only drink wine? What are we going to eat?" Her dress had dried, leaving many wrinkles. She straightened it as best she could and shook back her hair.

"I'll fish," he said dreamily, watching her. "Bass or salmon or something. Whatever swims in the ocean. I want to grill it over a beach bonfire."

"How manly of you." Ava smiled and went barefoot to the door to open it. Fragrant, clean air and bright sunshine streamed into her tiny house, and the sea shimmered like emeralds and sapphires below them.

The wood floor creaked as Bruno came to stand behind her. He put his arms around her waist. "Tell me you want a life like that too," he murmured into her hair and kissed her ear.

Ava let herself lean into his embrace, savoring the warmth of his body pressed against her own. She closed her eyes and let herself drift away from the sound of the waves crashing and the smell of salt in the air.

Bruno's arms tightened around her as he turned her to face him. He looked at her with intensity, his dark eyes reflecting something that made her heart skip a beat. "Do you still want a life with me, Ava?" he asked again, trailing one finger along her cheekbone, his gaze searching her face. "A life we build together?"

"Yes, I do want that," Ava murmured. "I've always wanted that."

Bruno took a deep breath and touched his forehead to hers before speaking. "I love you," he said in a voice barely above a whisper before once more kissing her on the lips.

CHAPTER 22

"Everything is ready for the boys. I can't wait for them to get here." With an impatient sigh, Billie sank into the wide, comfortable wicker chair in her cottage garden.

She had woken up with the sun. She prepared breakfast and cleaned the kitchen, made sure the boys' rooms upstairs were clean and aired and that their beds had fresh, lavender-scented sheets on them.

Ava closed her book and set it on the table. "Are you sure I shouldn't make myself invisible for a bit? I don't have a problem with that at all. You haven't seen your boys in weeks."

Billie smiled at the offer. "No, it's fine. I like having you here. And the boys will adore you just for keeping me company. They're happier when I'm not alone, even though I don't mind it. But I think it makes them feel guilty for not visiting more often."

"They're pretty busy, aren't they?"

Billie nodded. "Louis is in the last year of grad school. He is applying for jobs. So far, nothing has panned out yet."

"He's a marine biologist?"

"Yes, he is. I just hope that he won't move too far when he does find a job."

"It'll be okay," Ava said. "It's all about making it work. My daughter Zoe lives in Seattle, and I barely ever see her—sometimes I think we would try harder if we lived farther apart."

"You will, now."

Ava nodded. "I called her last night and left a message. She should know I'm going to stay in Mendocino Cove."

"Did you tell her about the house?"

"Not yet. I want to tell her in person."

"But did you show the house to Bruno yesterday?"

"I did."

"Did he like it? The storm must have hit you. Maybe the place wasn't at its best in the rain."

"He liked it anyway." Ava lowered her gaze to study her hands, a small smile playing on her lips.

Billie narrowed her eyes.

She'd been at Lizzie May University to talk with the biologist about an orphaned sea lion Billie had raised four years ago. The sea lion, Markus, was tagged for tracking. And after looking at the new data that had come in, they all went out for dinner together.

Ava had already been asleep when Billie came home, and there hadn't been time to talk about her trip to the arts and crafts home with Bruno.

Now, she wasn't exactly volunteering information.

"What happened to you?" Billie finally straight out asked. "You seem different today."

Ava primly crossed her legs, smoothing her blue linen skirt over her knees. "There's nothing different. Nothing happened."

"Sure," Billie said in her best *I don't believe you* voice. "*Something* happened. Hmm."

"No. Nothing. Don't worry about it." The corner of Ava's mouth twitched.

"You went to the house with Bruno..." Billie murmured, trying to piece it together. "No!" Her eyes flew open. Of course! That glow, that smile, the conjured look of innocence—"You *didn't*, Ava! Did you?" Her eyes widened with surprise. "Did you and your husband, uh...get reacquainted?"

"Um." Ava arranged her skirt some more, but then she laughed and looked up, eyes shining. "It was unbelievable, Billie."

"I thought you two were done and over with! Okay. Okay." Billie inhaled loudly and leaned back. "Don't leave me hanging. I want all the dirty details. Dish."

Ava chuckled. "There's nothing to dish. We got caught in the potting shed during the rain and uh...it was very romantic. *Very* romantic." A faint blush colored her cheeks.

"You're blushing. You, a wife and mother who's been around the block a few times, are blushing." Billie grinned.

"What do you mean, *around the block?*" Ava tried to look dignified, but then she smiled a sheepish smile. "Billie, what can I tell you? He was...uh, insistent. I've felt ignored for so long; I'm afraid it was a bit addictive to suddenly feel so desired. I simply couldn't say no." She sighed happily.

"Good for you." Billie chuckled. "You two are married, after all." Then she blinked wistfully. "I wish someone was insistent about desiring me. Too bad that train has sailed."

"Don't say that, Billie. I might be married, but I promise I thought the exact same thing." She shook her head. "The moment I decide I'm done, he does *that*. I didn't see it coming in a million years."

Billie nodded, but when her thoughts went to her ex-husband, there was no desire at all. Only old, deeply rooted anger.

"You all right?" Ava asked gently.

"I'm just quietly being envious over here." Billie closed her eyes and held her face into the warm sun. "But only a little. My love life is the least of my worries."

"Then what's the most of your worries?" Ava asked, interested.

Billie checked her watch. "Right now I worry that I'll get a call from Ben, saying his replacement is sick."

"His replacement at the animal hospital?"

"Yes. His friend promised to take over his duties for a couple of days."

"Is that the reason why your boys are suddenly coming for a visit?"

"Yes, that's right. It was an unexpected opportunity." It was rare that Ben, in particular, could get away from his duties as a vet for a large animal clinic. Louis was more flexible, at least with his time.

"Ben's picking up his brother because Louis doesn't have a car," Billie explained. "He doesn't need one in the city, but it also means he can't drive up here as often as he would like."

Ava smiled. "Maybe we should all pitch in for a birthday present."

Billie weaved her head. "I've thought about getting him one. It really doesn't make any sense financially, but it would also let Ben off the hook. He doesn't mind giving his brother a lift now and then, but it does add a lot of driving time to his trip here."

"There you go. Let's get Louis a car, and both boys will come and visit more often."

"Only of course Louis wouldn't accept a gifted car," Billie said, not at all certain her charming youngest wouldn't be delighted instead. She couldn't afford to buy one, even if she'd allow Ava, who clearly had a lot more spending money than herself, to pitch in. But it was good to have friends who cared.

Billie changed the topic before Ava could come up with a plan. "What do we have to do to get Zoe to come to Mendocino Cove?"

"I have no idea," Ava said slowly. "We'd have to work on her boyfriend first. He's older than she is, and I don't think Zoe was quite ready for the experience. She doesn't admit it, but I sense he doesn't like it when she and I meet too often."

"That's not good." Billie had liked the girlfriends her boys had introduced over the years. She couldn't imagine having one of them tell Ben or Louis not to come visit their mother.

"It's not," Ava said and picked up her phone. "Maybe this conversation is my sign to invite her to come here again."

"Keep bugging her," Billie agreed. "That's the ticket when it comes to recalcitrant children. Grown, own, or otherwise."

Ava giggled. "Recalcitrant," she repeated under her breath while texting her daughter.

The sound of a car engine and the faint crunching of tires in gravel drifted into the garden. "There they are!" Billie jumped up and hurried to the front door, opening it just as her boys got out of the car, handsome and smiling and waving hello.

"Hey, Mom!"

"Boys! Welcome!" She went out to meet them in the front yard. "Darling!" She threw her arms around Ben, who was in front. Dark and tall, he hugged her back, effortlessly lifting her feet off the ground.

"Put me down this instant," she said fondly. "And don't trample the daisies." She kissed his cheek and turned to her younger one. Louis was even taller than his brother, and with his stylish black-rimmed glasses and dirty-blond hair, he was the devastating spitting image of his father.

"Sweetheart!" She had to pull him down to kiss his cheek. Unlike his father, Louis was not a hugger. But he winked at her and pulled a bouquet of wildflowers from behind his back.

"For you, dearest mother," he said and handed them over. "We stopped and picked them along the way."

"They are...so pretty!"

"I told you to leave longer stems," Ben said good-humoredly. "Look, they're too short. Mom can barely keep the flowers together."

Louis pulled off his glasses and rubbed them clean with his T-shirt. "It's fine. It's fine, isn't it, Mom?" He put them on again, squinting at the flowers that had fallen to the ground, their stems indeed too short for Billie's hand.

"It's definitely fine," Billie agreed and adjusted her grip. Another wild daisy toppled to the ground, and she quickly kicked it into the bushes. "Come in, you two. Let's have a cup of coffee in the garden."

The boys followed her, chatting about the drive across the mountain range and Ben's car. Apparently, it reeked of dogs and cats and, possibly, goats. Ben maintained that it still smelled better than Louis's car would smell, if he had one. No doubt Louis would use it to transport fish and his old rubber boots and maybe even the octopuses he kept for his animal behavior research. Ben assured his brother they would drop clams all over the backseat while Louis was unsuccessfully trying to find his way up the mountain on his own.

Louis countered that at least they would ride with him while no self-respecting octopus would put their tank in Ben's stinking goat car, that Ben only wished he had patients as cool as octopuses, and that it was good he didn't since even Louis's dumbest octopus would immediately outsmart Ben and go buy his own car.

Billie listened happily to the laughter and the brotherly insults that flew back and forth in the kitchen while she finagled her short-stemmed flowers into a vase, brewed fresh coffee, and arranged platters of raspberry cheesecake and macarons. They carried everything outside where Ava was already standing, eager to finally meet her friend's children.

While the three of them were getting to know each other, sitting down and helping themselves to the treats, Billie quickly texted Jon.

Boys just got here. Bring Jenny and Audrey. Let's have cake together.

"What are you up to over there, Mom?" Ben had turned around and was smiling at her.

"I just told Uncle Jon you've arrived and to come have coffee and cake with us," Billie said.

Ava's phone pinged, and she pulled it out to glance at the screen. Surprised, she pulled back her chin, but the light that lit her eyes could only come from good news.

"What?" Billie asked eagerly.

"Zoe is coming to visit!" Ava said across the table. "She'll be here next week!"

"Next week," Billie murmured under her breath and gave Ava a thumbs-up. Maybe she could get the boys to come up again... "Excellent."

"What was that, Mom?" Louis looked up from his slice of cheesecake. "What's excellent?

"The cake, dear. Your uncle's new recipe. Don't you think it is good?" Billie said and folded her hands.

"It's the best. Especially after having to eat at the diner at my place the last two days. Yesterday they served mystery meat surprise for dinner, and the day before it was sludgy slaw soup. Though both meals had the same peculiar sour aftertaste. So maybe it was the same thing."

"Mm-hmm, that sounds good. Tell me more about it, sweetheart," Billie said distractedly. "What do they serve for breakfast?"

While her son talked, Billie settled deeper into her chair and put the tips of her fingers together.

Audrey, Louis, Ben, and soon, Zoe...four lonely young people who needed love and stability and good food in their lives.

It really was a no-brainer.

Her eyes met Ava's across the table. Without saying a word, they nodded.

It was time to introduce the kids to each other.

CHAPTER 23

I hear a car! That must be Billie and her boys!" Jenny clapped the flour off her hands, glad to get away from the minor baking task allocated to her.

She couldn't make a cupcake for the life of her, not even the ones from boxes with two-step instructions on them. But Audrey had plotted a scheme to teach her basic skills. Jenny hadn't found the heart to tell her daughter that no, not everybody could be whatever they wanted when they grew up. Sometimes, it was best to just give up and go have a glass of wine on the beach. "I can't wait to meet Billie's boys!" Jenny exclaimed too gleefully, happy to get away.

Her daughter eyed her from the other side of the kitchen. The sleeves of her pretty yellow summer dress were folded up as far as they would go, and her arms were sunk elbow-deep in the dough that filled Grandma Rosie's galaxy-sized mixing bowl. "Nice, Mom," Audrey said dryly. "I know what you're doing—hey! Careful!"

"Oops." Enthusiastically slinging her apron on the counter, Jenny had accidentally knocked over a massive bag of powdered sugar. Toppling over, it flung its white contents across the entire floor to the kitchen door like a celebrity drug lord. More still hovered in the air, slowly weaving toward the ground like snow.

"Sheesh, Mom." Audrey started to laugh, then emerged from her bowl and tossed Jenny a clean kitchen towel with little bears on it. "Here. Best to clean up a bit."

The doorbell chimed just as Jenny caught the towel. "Thank you, Audrey." Jenny grinned and dabbed at her clothes, turning to make her way to the foyer "Don't worry about cleaning it up, darling. I'm going to do it later."

"I'll do it when I'm done with my cookies," Audrey called after her. "Be careful you don't slip in the sugar!"

"What a way to go, right?" Jenny called back and hightailed it out of the kitchen to open the door. "Hello!"

"Hello there," Billie said and waved her sons closer. "Here we are. This is Ben," she pointed at an incredibly good-looking young man with dark hair and dark eyes.

With a huge smile, Jenny stepped aside so Ben could enter. "I'm so pleased to meet you, Ben," she said. To her delight, Ben held out a formal hand, and solemnly they shook.

"I've heard so much about you," he said, but the glimmer of humor in his eyes reminded Jenny very much of her own River. Ben was pulling either her leg or his mother's with the formal greeting.

"I see." She laughed. "You have to write it all down for me sometime," she said and waved him inside. "I'd sure like to get all the details."

"Anytime." He came inside. "What an absolutely marvelous house you have."

She chuckled. "It's lovely to meet you. Call me Jenny."

"Thank you, Jenny." Ben grinned and turned to wait for the others.

"And this is my younger one, Louis," Billie said happily.

"Ah, the marine biologist, isn't it?" Like his brother, Louis was handsome, but where his brother was dark, he was light. Louis, too, offered his hand and shook.

"That's right," he said good-humoredly. "Since Mom always made me feed her rescue pelicans, I thought I might as well make a job out of it."

Jenny smiled. "I thought you were researching the behavior of octopuses."

"I am indeed. They eat the same food as the pelicans, though." He smiled and offered an aluminum-foil-covered plate. "Mom made these to bring."

"Thank you very much, Billie. Come on in."

"Louis, darling, bring the plate into the kitchen, will you?" Billie asked before Jenny could take the offering. "Jenny and I will get the rest from the car."

"The kitchen to your right, behind the foyer," Jenny called out. "And if you keep straight down the corridor, you'll find the patio and the beach. Go on ahead, we'll be there in a minute."

"All right." Louis turned to his brother. "Go ahead. I just want to wash my hands. I'll meet you at the beach," he said, and he and Ben disappeared.

"I love them already, Billie," Jenny said and hugged her friend. "Where's Ava? Did she not want to come?"

Billie smiled enigmatically. "Ava and her husband are coming in a while," she said. "Bruno picked her up earlier to sign the closing documents for the house."

"What's that smile about?" Jenny asked as they walked through the warmth of the afternoon to Billie's pickup truck.

Billie let down the tailgate and pulled the cooler to her. "Between you and me and Ava, she's making up with her husband," she whispered. "I'd say it's going well!"

"Are they really?" Jenny's heart lifted. "Did she change her mind?"

"I think it's him who changed his mind," Billie said. "Here, help me get this down."

Together, they set the heavy cooler on the ground.

"Did he? Like how?" Jenny wanted to know.

"He's fixing up the house for her," Billie confided. "He's finally woken up to the reality of losing her, and it seems to be the last thing he wants. I'd say..." She opened the cooler to check the contents. "I'd say it's going swimmingly. I almost didn't recognize Ava when I saw her after the meeting with Bruno. Ten years younger, I'm telling you."

"Ah." Jenny knew about the fountain of youth effect that love had. She, too, felt decades younger with Jon.

"I know." Billie sighed. "I'm preaching to the choir. I'll have to find myself a boy toy just to keep up with everyone getting hitched left, right, and center."

Jenny giggled at the thought. "I'll let you know if I see any," she promised. "What did you bring?"

"Marinated tri-tip steak for grilling." Billie pointed. "Shrimp skewers and Santa Maria-style BBQ chicken with corn. Jon was going to bring watermelon-feta salad and pineapple slices to grill." She closed the lid again.

"Audrey is baking cupcakes and macadamia cookies and who knows what all," Jenny said and hauled the cooler into her arms. "We once again are not going to starve. But Billie—you don't always have to make so much. We can just have hamburgers for a change."

Billie looked at her, deadpan. "Maybe when I find myself a man. Until then, I'll have to channel my energy into grocery shopping and providing food, I'm afraid."

It made Jenny laugh enough that she had to set the cooler back down. "Poor Billie," she said when she recovered. "How about Miles? He likes you. Maybe you two should go have a coffee."

"Who?" Billie pulled the second cooler down and slammed the tailgate back up.

"Miles. The jazz musician professor from Lizzie May," Jenny said. Together, they waddled toward the door with their heavy loads. "He gets that look in his eyes when you're around, and I swear he eats dinner at Jon's just for a chance to see you."

"Miles. That's right." Billie weaved her head. "The fact that he hasn't occurred to me as an option is not a good sign. I'm not sure I'm attracted to him."

"Ava wanted to divorce her husband," Jenny pointed out. "I don't think she was very attracted to *him* when she first arrived in Mendocino Cove."

"But she is now," Billie countered and pushed the door to the hotel open with her shoulder. "And how! You should have seen the googly eyes they made at each other when he picked her up. Don't tell her I said that."

Jenny giggled and followed her friend inside, pushing the door closed with her foot behind her.

CHAPTER 24

"Hush!" Billie stopped dead. She set down her cooler, waving Jenny to do the same and join her.

Jenny tiptoed to where Billie stood by the kitchen door and peeked inside.

Louis was standing with his back to them while Audrey was cutting cookies from her dough and rolling out more, focused on what she was doing. Clearly, she hadn't noticed Louis.

He cleared his throat. "Ahem."

Startled, she looked up.

Billie put a hand to her heart, and even Jenny had to smile. Her daughter looked adorable with her smudge of flour on the cheek, her hair messily tied into a short ponytail, and her apron showing off her figure.

Obviously, Louis thought the same. "Hi," he said.

"Hi." Audrey glanced at Billie and Jenny peeking around the corner and smiled, shaking her head at them. She was smart enough to read their expressions for what they were.

"I'm Louis, Billie's son," Louis said winsomely.

"Right. The marine biologist, isn't it? I'm Audrey, Jenny's daughter," Audrey said and resumed her task. "Can I help you with anything? A glass of water?"

Billie leaned against one side of the door frame, and Jenny against the other. No way were they going to miss this.

"Oh, no, I'm fine." Louis ran a hand through his hair. "Erm." He looked at the mess on the floor. The powdered sugar lay undisturbed, not quite glittering like snow, but not far from it either.

Audrey glanced at it too but didn't offer an explanation. "How is the marine biology going?" she asked after a while. A small smile was playing around her lips.

"They say the ocean is vast and full of wonders, but I never expected to find something as enchanting as you in this kitchen."

Audrey looked up. "Really? That's your best line?" She put a hand on her waist and laughed.

"I have more." Louis didn't seem to be perturbed by the fit of laughter. "Sorry for the intrusion, but I couldn't resist the sweet aroma—both from your oven and your presence."

"Eww! I don't *smell*." Audrey, who had just caught herself, started to laugh again.

Louis chuckled. "If my calculations are correct, your baking skills emit a gravitational pull stronger than any ocean current."

"Just—no."

"Excuse the intrusion, but you've got a way of making marine biology seem bland compared to the magic happening in this kitchen."

"Thanks. That's probably enough of that." Smiling, Audrey held up a hand. "What really brought you into the kitchen?" she asked, rubbing her cheek with her wrist and only smearing the flour around. "Do you want something to drink?"

"Thanks, but no," he said. "I wanted to show you my research. Are you interested in some really first-class octopus data?" He pulled out his phone and wiggled it temptingly.

Again, Audrey had to laugh. She set the roller pin aside and crossed her arms, leaning against the counter. "You can show it to me, but I think I should point out that both our mothers are standing in the door, watching you."

Louis turned and executed a polite half-bow before turning back.

Jenny laughed herself, but Billie only shook her head. "Why don't you let Audrey finish her cookies so she can join us?" she asked her son.

"What about my research?" He looked over his shoulder and raised an eyebrow. "Mother, don't you think it's very important?"

"Audrey, just tell him to stop when you're fed up," Billie said. "He'll let you get on with it."

"It's all right," Audrey said good-humoredly. "Louis, I'd love to see your octopus. Show me, and then help me finish baking these. It's your punishment for being silly and making me late."

"That turned out better than I'd hoped," Louis said and lifted his phone.

"Louis, careful with your elbow!" Jenny called out.

Too late—Louis knocked over an open jar, sending sprinkles flying all over the floor. They rained down on top of the powdered sugar, creating a colorful mess. "Ah!" Louis startled. "I'm sorry, Audrey."

Audrey tilted her head as she regarded the floor. "It's a masterpiece," she said seriously. "So pretty."

He ran a hand through his hair. "I'll clean it up. Do you have a broom and dustpan?" He looked around. "Over there? Is that a broom clo—" Striding toward the broom closet, Louis stepped into the mess of powder and sprinkles. His foot slipped, his leg shot up at a sharp angle, and before he had time to protest, he landed with a smack on his bottom.

Billie and Jenny both stared in shock, but Audrey silently bent at the middle, laughing so hard she couldn't catch her breath.

"Funny," Louis said from where he was sitting, brushing off sprinkles and powdered sugar.

"Audrey!" Jenny said finally. "Really!"

Audrey bit her lip to squelch her amusement. She put down her rolling pin and stepped carefully into the sugary mess to hold out a hand. "Take my hand," she said. "No point in sitting there and waiting for the sprinkles to stain your khakis."

With a smile, Louis took her hand and stood. "Not the impression I meant to make," he noted as he shook the last sprinkles off his bottom.

"You don't need to make an impression," Audrey said in a kind voice. "I'm absolutely desperate for friends my age. Let's clean this up together real quick. I want to finish the last tray of cookies so I can meet everyone outside."

Jenny waved Billie back to where they'd left their coolers. They brought them into the kitchen and put the meats and seafood and fruit into the fridge while the kids cleaned the floor and talked about cupcakes and jellyfish.

Jenny made everyone a piña colada, and then she and Billie went outside, leaving Audrey and Louis to get better acquainted.

"Do you think they'll marry?" Billie asked hopefully when they stepped on the patio.

"Definitely," Jenny said. "They just had a proper meet-cute, didn't they? They're practically contractually obligated to get hitched."

Ben joined them. "Where's my brother?" he asked. "He's young and impressionable, and I like to make sure he doesn't get himself into trouble."

"Too late. He's in the kitchen, talking to Jenny's daughter, Audrey," Billie said and took a long sip from her glass.

"Go ahead and get yourself a drink too," Jenny said. "There's plenty. The kitchen is right behind the foyer."

"Don't mind if I do," Ben murmured and left.

"Well..." With a slight frown pulling on her forehead, Billie looked after her eldest. "Not that it matters, but when is Zoe getting here again?"

Jenny laughed. "Not today, I don't think. Come on, Billie, you're not actually serious about the kids marrying, are you? It's all just fun."

Billie looked at her for a long moment. "Of course," she said then. "Of course it's all just fun."

CHAPTER 25

The afternoon sun was starting its slow descent toward the ocean, casting a warm golden glow across the beach and cliffs beyond. Ava sat in the garden of the cottage, her brand-new easel before her.

Earlier in the week, she had signed the papers and stopped by the arts and crafts house to take possession of her house officially. Ava had felt giddy with joy and radiant as a field of blooming sunflowers when she entered her beautiful house—legally, from now on.

It had been hers in the past, and now it was hers again. It felt marvelous to own something she had loved all her life. She never knew how much she had missed her home until she had it back.

Happy as a child dancing in rain showers, she'd skipped through the house, waving the deed in her hand, and, she was now a little embarrassed to say, utterly disregarding her promise to be careful.

It was only when a loose ceiling tile in the upstairs corridor fell with a thud right before her feet that she had come to her senses. By the time Bruno caught up with her, she was already on her way back downstairs, unscathed and unapologetic.

She and Bruno had enjoyed a picnic lunch of savory quiche and cool white wine in the magical, wild backyard. Lying on the blanket between the vines and wildflowers, Bruno had turned to look at her as if she was the only thing in the world that could hold his interest.

Ava had lain down beside him and blinked at her husband's face, the handsome dark eyes that for so long had seemed not to see her.

Now they did. Now she was his one and only focus.

She smiled and trailed the outline of Bruno's jaw with the tip of her finger, letting it come to rest on his mouth.

"I love you, Ava," he said in a husky voice, his lips moving against her finger. He grabbed her hand and pressed the open palm to his lips. Slowly, he trailed kisses down the inside of her arm while Ava closed her eyes and exhaled softly.

"I feel the same way, Bruno," she whispered.

Bruno leaned over her and kissed her tenderly, murmuring words of adoration as their surroundings became a blur around them. The sweet scent of the wildflowers, the gentle rustle of the vines in the breeze, all faded away as they lay amongst nature's beauty.

What happened between them erased Ava's last lingering doubts that Bruno was not serious about her.

Bruno had always been a good lover. But after finally casting off the yoke of his business and deciding to build the life he truly wanted—a life full of beauty and love and companionship—he left Ava breathless, gasping with pleasure she'd not known before.

As the memories came back to her, Ava stopped painting her seascape. Heat crawled up her neck and, smiling, she shook her head at herself. Then she resolutely squared her shoulders and dipped her brush into first one blue, then another, to mix the perfect shade and daubed it onto the canvas.

The picnic was one week ago.

Two weeks ago, she was going to get a divorce. She drew boundaries and took action to shape a new, happier life for herself. Ava knew what a life without Bruno would look like and was no longer afraid of it. She no longer depended on him for her own happiness. Was it a coincidence that now, she also was more in love with her husband than ever—and he with her?

The same night of the picnic, Bruno had flown back to Seattle. He was going to arrange for a company to pack up what they wanted from their old house for the new one in Mendocino Cove. The next morning, he had returned with his tools and hard helmet and set to work repairing their house. He knew what he wanted, and he knew what he was doing. Never before had contractors worked so quickly.

Ava tried to concentrate on her task and the stunning landscape before her. "I'll not finish this painting by the time he's fixed the house if I go on like this," she murmured.

She had always loved her father's studio by the sea. Stepping into that space again and remembering the many brushes and paints and easels that used to be

194   NELLIE BROOKS

there had inspired Ava to try her hand at painting the view he had so often captured on canvas.

Someone had to keep painting all this beauty.

The blue looked good. Goodish. A little flat. How did he make the water sparkle so brilliantly? Ava let her brush sink and critically tilted her head. Then she had to smile at herself. What had she expected? The skills of a professional, absorbed by osmosis from watching Dad in her childhood?

As she sat there, with her watercolor set on the small table in front of her, she couldn't help but feel a sense of freedom wash over her. So she had inherited her father's love for painting, not his talent. His paintings were beautiful creations of colors and shapes infused with feelings. Hers looked like a dolphin had used his left flipper. It didn't matter. Maybe with lots of practice and patience, she would eventually produce something acceptable. Maybe not.

Life wasn't always about reaching a goal. Sometimes, it was just about painting because painting felt good.

Maybe spots of sea foam on the waves would make the water look more vivid.

Ava dipped her brush into the water and then into the paint, watching as the colors spread across the paper in surprising ways. She smiled as she continued to paint, her mind drifting to thoughts of her new house.

Besides overlooking the contractors he had hired, Bruno added charming new details Ava loved. He had offered her a choice selection of shades for the up-stairs walls and had spent hours sanding and sealing the wooden floors to make them shine. He'd ordered beautiful vintage doorknobs from an antique shop and polished the seahorse door knocker just to see Ava smile. He'd even ordered handmade stained-glass panels, matching the ones downstairs, to add windows above the fireplace mantel in their bedroom.

Ava decided to leave the sea be and try her hand at the cliffs in the distance and the flowers in the foreground. There wasn't much difference between the shapes of her flowers and her cliffs, but she was having fun and that was all that mattered.

Lost in her thoughts, Ava didn't hear the sound of a car approaching until someone called out. She turned to see who it was and caught a glimpse of a slim figure with long, dark hair walking toward her.

"Zoe! You're here already? You arrived earlier than I expected!" Ava stood to hug her daughter, who despite her flight and the long drive from the airport over the mountain, smelled of almonds and roses.

"I caught an earlier flight and thought I'd surprise you." Zoe smiled and stepped back to look at Ava. "Mom, what are you doing?"

Ava smiled and put down her brush. She looked down at her watercolor painting, then back up at Ava. "Just painting," she said, feeling a little self-conscious. "Really I was waiting for you to get here."

"What are you painting?"

Ava turned the easel toward Zoe, revealing the landscape she had been working on. "It's the view from a bluff, just like your grandpa used to paint. Of course, he painted the one from our old garden, not Billie's."

Zoe's eyes widened in amazement. "It looks just like his paintings! You're talented, Mom."

"No." Ava had to laugh. "It really doesn't look anything like his, Zoe. But thank you for saying that."

Zoe sat down next to her. "Can I try?" she asked, pointing at the watercolor set.

"Of course," Ava said, passing the set and a fresh canvas to her daughter.

"I've been thinking a lot about Grandpa and Grandma while I was driving over the mountains," Zoe said. "I miss them, and this is the perfect release." She took the brush and began to paint, her strokes confident and sure.

Ava watched in amazement as her daughter created a beautiful watercolor painting of the view. It was clear that it was Zoe who had inherited her grandfather's talent for painting. A sense of pride washed over Ava. "How do you know how to do that, darling? It's beautiful."

"Two of Grandpa's paintings hang in my bedroom," Zoe murmured as she added the finishing highlights. "Every night, I imagined myself sitting at that bluff by the sea where he sat, painting peacefully. It calms me down. That's how I fall asleep."

"Well, you imagined yourself right into a new skill." Ava looked over Zoe's shoulder. "I love painting as a creative outlet, but I'm a better writer."

"Yes, you are," Zoe agreed. "I always hoped you'd take that up again."

Ava nodded. "I've played with the idea since coming here. I could contact a few magazines and pitch some articles."

Zoe turned to look at her. "You could write about the house. You said Grandma used to have visitors who had read about it in magazines."

"That's a great idea. Hmm. I'll think about it." Absent-mindedly, Ava started to gather her daughter's long, dark hair into her hands, braiding it into a long braid while Zoe finished her painting. When she reached the end, Ava looked at what she was doing. "I'm sorry, Zoe. I didn't notice what my hands were doing."

"No worries. I still like when you do it. It reminds me of being a schoolgirl, drinking hot cocoa and eating toast in the kitchen while you're doing my hair," Zoe said. She pulled a hairband off her wrist and handed it to her mother. "I might as well leave the braid in. My flyaways are driving me nuts in the sea breeze."

With a smile, Ava slipped the hairband onto the end of the long, heavy braid and laid it over Zoe's shoulder. Her daughter had inherited all of Bruno's Roman beauty.

"Thanks." Zoe washed out her brush. It had taken her only a few minutes to create a picture ten times more beautiful than Ava's efforts. "You know," Zoe said suddenly, looking at her canvas, "I think I should try this more often. I enjoy it."

Ava bent down and pressed a kiss on her daughter's head. "Me too. Let's paint together from the same spot where Grandpa used to stand."

Zoe looked up at her. "Can we do that? I thought they sold that magical house of theirs a long time ago."

Ava sat in the chair beside Zoe and took her hands into her own. "I bought it back," she said, only barely suppressing her excitement.

Slowly, a huge smile spread over her daughter's face. "Mom! You really bought it back, didn't you? You did! I can tell from the look in your eyes!"

Ava nodded. "I'm so thrilled."

"I'm..." Zoe stood. "Mom. I've always wanted to see the house. Grandma talked about it all the time, telling me stories... I've *always* wanted to see it."

"Well." Ava stood as well. "Let's go over there right now. What do you think?"

"Sure. But, um, now that you have your own house and all..." Zoe folded her fingers together and took a deep breath. "What about Dad?" she asked, exhaling. "I meant to ask you for a while now, Mom. Are you leaving him?"

Ava blinked. Zoe was busy leading her own life. She had a complicated boyfriend, worked long hours in a bakery, and was planning to open her own soon. Not in a hundred years had Ava expected Zoe to notice her parents' marriage wasn't perfect.

Ava took a deep breath, but then she had to laugh at the expression in her daughter's eyes. "Do you *want* me to leave him?"

"I want you to be happy, Mom," Zoe said seriously. "I feel so bad thinking about you alone at home or meeting with your first-wife club..."

Ava leaned forward. "My what? My first-wife club?"

"Yeah. You know, like the ones that always get divorced?"

Ava fell back again. "Best not to tell my friends you're calling us that, darling. Also, Dad is here in Mendocino Cove. I thought you knew."

"No." Zoe's eyes widened. "No, I haven't heard from him."

Ava smiled and took her daughter's hand. "Let's go see him, okay?"

Zoe's lip first pressed into a tight line, then relaxed into a small smile. "Really?"

Ava nodded. "Really. He's quit work and golfing and followed me here."

"He *followed* you?" Zoe tilted her head in disbelief. "Is Dad going to *stay* here with you?"

"I think so," Ava said and smiled. "I think that's what he means to do. We're bringing some of the furniture from the Seattle home down. We might sell the Seattle house too. But that's not decided yet."

Zoe swallowed and looked at her feet, then back at her mother. "I'm so happy," she said quietly. "You have no idea how happy that makes me, Mom. I thought..."

"Me too," Ava said quickly. "I thought so too. But I didn't twist his arm. This is what he wants to do."

"And you believe him?" Zoe asked, her eyes glued to her mom.

"I believe him," Ava confirmed. "And what's more important, I love him. And he loves me."

"He said that?" Zoe whispered.

"Yes, Zoe. He did say that." Ava pulled Zoe into a hug. Adult or not, kids wanted their parents to love each other. How long had Zoe carried doubts about her parents' happiness? It was a heavy weight at any age, to think a loved one was lonely or trapped in a troubled relationship.

"That's good." For a moment, Zoe rested her head on Ava's shoulder. Then she straightened. "Let's go see Grandma's house. I can't wait another second."

"The house was neglected for a long time," Ava warned Zoe. "It doesn't look its best right now."

"But?" Zoe smiled. Her pretty almond-shaped dark eyes shone as all the good news sank in.

"But Dad's fixing it up," Ava promised. "For me and you and himself."

"We are still a family, then," Zoe said slowly.

Her grandmother had often had that look when she looked at her garden and the flowers swaying in front of the sapphire ocean.

"We are a family," Ava confirmed.

CHAPTER 26

Ava packed up the painting supplies while Zoe went inside to meet Billie, who was busy in the kitchen, and introduced herself.

Then Zoe and Ava hopped into Ava's car and drove the short distance to the house, the anticipation building with each passing moment. As they parked the car and got out, Ava could see the excitement in Zoe's eyes.

"Wow, it really does look amazing," Zoe said as they approached the house. "What a wonderful old house you grew up in, Mom. And Dad's done an excellent job because it doesn't look neglected at all!"

Ava smiled, feeling a sense of pride at her husband's handiwork. As they walked around the house, she pointed out all the charming details that Bruno had added, from hand-carved brackets to restored columns and new window boxes on the front porch.

"All that in a week," she said. "He really knows what he's doing. If it had been me, these repairs would have lasted months, if not years."

"He's got his contacts," Zoe said and picked a flower to tuck behind her ear. "This sun makes me not want to go back to Seattle."

"Hey! Zoe! Ava!" Bruno came from the garden to meet them, wiping his hands on a bandanna. "Fancy seeing you two here." He laughed and caught his daughter in a one-armed hug, pressing a kiss on her temple.

"Hi, Dad. I haven't seen you in ages." Zoe hugged him back. "I hear you're planning on letting other people get a chance at the firm for once?"

"Not only planning." He let go of his daughter and went to pull Ava into his arms, kissing her on the lips. "I'm out. I'm never using a golf course as an office again."

Zoe smiled up at him. "Hear, hear," she said softly. "That's good news. You've worked long enough, and I think you should enjoy yourself and keep Mom company."

"That is the plan." He smiled at Ava, and she smiled back.

"It looks fantastic, Dad. How is everything going here?"

"Great." He pulled Ava closer, squeezing her tight before letting her go. "Do you two want a tour? They just finished the roof, and the ceiling inside is finally fixed too. Tomorrow, the Millers will swap out some of the old plumbing pipes. The truck with the furniture arrived today, and it's all waiting for you to arrange it, honey."

"Really?"

"Really. We're ready to move in." He looked at her. "Good?"

"Fabulous." She smiled at him. "Thank you, Bruno." Something had changed between them. They were equals now.

"Come *on*!" Zoe was already halfway to the front door.

"Hear her?" Bruno put an arm around Ava's waist, and they followed their daughter. "She sounds like she's fifteen again."

"It's not that long ago that she was fifteen," Ava remarked and walked up the steps. "It's easy to forget, isn't it?"

He shook his head, a small frown between his eyes. "I missed so much, Ava," he murmured. "I'm only just realizing how much."

"Mom, give us the grand tour," Zoe said and stepped aside so Ava could open the front door. "I want to see the house through your eyes. Tell me about every room."

"Oh, dear. Starting when?" Ava laughed and turned the brass knob. She went into the glorious living room, telling her stories of the time a baseball smashed the precious stained-glass window, of the swing Dad had mounted for her on the beam crossing the ceiling, about the epic battles she and Billie had fought up and down the unusual, freestanding staircase, using empty cardboard tubes meant for shipping paintings as makeshift swords.

Slowly, their little family made their way through the art studios and the rest of the downstairs.

"The wood floors are beautiful," Ava said when they looked into the downstairs main bedroom. It used to be her parents' but now would be hers and Bruno's.

Zoe went into the attached bathroom to admire the freestanding tub and the new fixtures and cabinets Ava had picked out.

"Ava? I found something between the baseboard and the wall," Bruno said quietly and pulled her aside. "Look."

Ava's heart skipped a beat. "What did you find?"

Bruno reached into his pocket and pulled out a small gold ring. It was delicate and simple, with a stunning diamond in the center.

Ava recognized it immediately—it was her mother's ring, the one that the family had thought was lost forever. Mom had cried for days when she lost it until Dad had painted her ring and hung the painting over her bed to console her. After that, Mom was still sad but had to laugh every time she thought of her lost wedding ring.

"It's my mother's! Where did you find it?" Ava asked, a sense of disbelief washing over her.

"Right here. It was wedged behind the old baseboard molding," Bruno said. "The diamond was pointing down, so I didn't see it until I removed the entire board."

"It fell behind the bed," Ava said. "Mom swore she'd put it on the nightstand. It must've hit the floor and bounced right into the crack between the board and the wall!"

"Yes, I thought something like that happened," Bruno said. "Though I didn't know it was your mother's."

"Before that, it belonged to my dad's mom, my grandmother," Ava said. "I have almost nothing to remind me of her, but I know she loved this ring. It was handed down to her too. It's very old."

"Are you guys okay?" Zoe asked and crossed past them out of the room. "I'm going to check out upstairs. Is there a room for me too?"

"We'll be there in a minute, sweetheart," Ava called after her. "Pick whichever room you like."

She still couldn't believe it.

The ring was a family heirloom that she thought was gone forever. A lump formed in her throat as she looked at Bruno, holding the golden band.

"It's so delicate," he said quietly. Then he looked up. "I noticed you took off your wedding band, Ava."

"Oh. Yes, I did." Ava smiled, feeling embarrassed and ashamed at her pettiness. To her surprise, a tear fell from her eye when she blinked. "I left it in Seattle for you to find, Bruno. I'm sorry."

"Not as sorry as I am," he said. "But don't worry. That marriage is over."

She blinked another tear away so she could see him better. "What do you mean?"

"We have a new marriage now," he said softly. "A better marriage. I promise to do all I can to make you happy." He cupped her face in his hand, rubbing his thumb over her cheek and wiping away her tears.

"I promise as well." Ava looked from the ring to her husband's dark eyes. "Finders keepers, Bruno," she whispered.

"If it's mine to give, I give it to you. Will you wear it, Ava?" Bruno asked, his voice low.

Ava nodded. She had to quietly clear her throat before she could answer. "Yes. I will," she said, holding out her hand.

Bruno took her hand and slipped the ring onto her finger. It fit as if it had been made for her. Ava looked down at the ring, feeling overwhelmed with emotion. She turned to Bruno and threw her arms around him, pulling him in for a deep, passionate kiss.

Bruno wrapped his arms around her, kissing her back with equal passion. "Ava," he whispered, breaking away from her lips. "When you do that, I want more than just to kiss you."

Ava felt a familiar warmth spread through her body at his words. She smiled as desire washed over her. "I want that too," she whispered back. "But this isn't the time."

"No, I suppose not." He exhaled. "I meant to ask," he said, looking down to catch her gaze. "Have you gained weight?"

Ava narrowed her eyes, but her husband's embrace told her she was safe. "It's Billie's cooking," she exclaimed. "It's too good to say no. I have dieted for so long I can't do it anymore. Or rather, I don't want to do it anymore."

"Whatever it is you're doing, I love it. I love how you feel," he murmured. "I love your curves and your warmth, your sensuality and allure. I don't know how I kept my hands off you, but I hope you don't mind if I make up for the time we lost."

Ava smiled. "Generally, I don't mind."

The sound of footsteps on the stairs brought them back to the moment. Ava and Bruno pulled away from each other, turning to see Zoe coming down the stairs, a curious look on her face.

"What's going on? Why are you still in here?" Zoe asked, looking around.

Ava looked at Bruno, then back at Zoe. "Oh, nothing. We were just admiring the ring Dad found."

Zoe's eyes widened in excitement. "What ring? Can I see it?"

Ava held out her hand, showing Zoe the delicate gold ring on her finger. "It was my grandmother's and then my mother's. She lost it when I was little. Dad found it hidden in a crack by the wall."

Zoe gasped in amazement. "That's incredible! I can't believe you got it back."

"I can't believe it either," Ava said. "We thought it was lost forever. But it was still there, hidden and waiting for its time."

"It looks good on you." Zoe smiled.

"Let's go outside," Bruno said. "It's a beautiful evening. Let's show Zoe the beach. The stairs down the bluff are brand-new."

"You have a *beach*?" Zoe spread her hands as if she should have been informed about the beach a long time ago. "No one ever mentioned a beach. Mom?"

"Are you sure it never came up? I'm sure it must have." Ava had to laugh at her daughter's face. "Maybe you got all the beaches in my stories mixed up. Well—that, and we only really have a beach when the tide is low."

"Works for me." Zoe sighed. "I wish I could retire here with you." She turned toward the living room.

Ava and Bruno started walking too. "What about Seattle?" Ava asked carefully. Was her daughter serious about wanting to live here too?

Zoe weaved her head but didn't reply.

"You know, darling, you can always move here," Ava said gently. "Of course Dad and I would love nothing more."

"Move in with you?" Zoe looked at them over her shoulder with a smile. "Are you sure?"

"Sure we're sure," Bruno confirmed. "You always have a home with us. You can also look for your own place in town, of course. There are some nice houses for sale. Nothing with a beach, though, but there are beautiful public beaches and plenty of coastline."

"Well, I would need a job too," Zoe said and pushed open the sliding door.

It wasn't much of a protest. Ava looked at Bruno. He raised his eyebrows.

"You could finally open your own bakery," Ava said as they went outside. "Mendocino Cove doesn't have one yet."

"It doesn't?"

"No, not even one."

"Hmm. I can't move right this second, but lately I have been thinking it is time to stop working for others and start my own business. I'll look into Mendocino Cove as a location. At least it'll be a reason to visit!"

The sun was just beginning to set over the ocean. Streaks of gold and fire glowed above the water and the faraway cliffs.

"Wait. Is this your *garden*?" Zoe asked in disbelief. "I thought at first it was a wilderness. But there are paths." She went ahead, calling out her discoveries of the fruit trees, the koi pond, and all the other little things her grandparents had hidden among the overgrown flower beds. Then she exclaimed over the restored steps leading to the beach and, climbing down, vanished from sight.

Following her to the stairs, Ava ran her fingers through the feathery leaves of ponytail grass. "She's right. It barely is a garden anymore. I have a lot to keep me busy here," she said and let her gaze wander over the neglected garden.

Bruno slid an arm around her waist. "We have worked enough. Let's give someone else a chance."

Ava chuckled at his echo of Zoe's earlier comment. "And are you going to pay for it?"

"Of course. I almost lost you over my work. The least it can do is pay for making up lost time now."

"All right," Ava said and smiled up at him. "But only the first do-over. After that, I'm taking care of my own garden."

Bruno smiled back. "I'll drink coffee and watch you."

Ava swatted playfully at him, and he laughed and pulled her to him. "What I meant to say of course is that I'll help you," he murmured into her hair. "At your command, my lady."

"Well...maybe you can hire help now and then," she conceded. "After all, we'll need plenty of time for other things."

"We'll do that," he said and kissed her until Ava was breathless, and Zoe was calling for them to come down to the beach.

CHAPTER 27

W hat about this one?" Jenny asked and ducked out of the glorious sun of an August day into the shade of an oak tree. They had caught the ferry to Mendocino Island. The island was popular with tourists and locals alike for its gardens, pretty harbors, flowers, and sea-salt chocolates. The small towns of Mariglen and Rosehaven were the main attractions in the west, and sprinkled along the East Coast lay Alveridge, Avelock, and Alver.

Of all the small towns, Aver was the biggest by far. It had the only freshwater spring on the island. The spring fed the bubbling creek that gave the town its name, and the Aver was proudly crossed by no fewer than five tiny bridges whose wrought-iron scrollwork carried countless lovers' locks.

Because the town also had an adorable historical church, a tiny but modern synagogue, two charming sand beaches, and several outlook spots on cliffs that were framed naturally by ancient storybook trees, Aver was a popular spot for weddings. The street behind the most elaborate little bridge decorated with the most locks was aptly named Lover's Lane. Lover's Lane always attracted a crowd because here, one pretty bridal shop bumped against the next.

"Ava, that store does look cute." Faye joined Jenny and waved Billie over too.

"What's this?"

"A vintage wedding dress boutique," Billie said. "I've never seen it before. It must be new."

"The dresses in the window are stunning." Faye dreamily put a hand on her no longer perfectly flat belly, and Jenny smiled. Every mother recognized the protective gesture.

"Beautifully preserved dresses from past eras," Billie read the lettering on the window. "Ava? What do you think? Should we have lunch first?"

"It looks interesting, and I haven't found anything that knocks me off my feet yet," Ava said cheerfully. "Let's go in and see what they have."

Jenny opened the door, and a small golden bell dinged above them.

"Hello." A young woman of about Audrey's age looked up from her phone and smiled.

"Hi." Jenny smiled back as her friends poured into the small store. It was an enchanting mix of gleaming old wood and soft light filtered through windows and skylights.

When everyone was inside, the young woman stood. "Welcome. I'm Hazel. How can I help you?"

"My husband and I are having a recommitment ceremony," Ava explained. "I'm looking for a dress. Nothing too fancy, but obviously I'd like it to look nice. And, uh, slimming. Maybe a fitted bodice? I've gained a bit of weight lately."

Billie rolled her eyes, but Faye gave her a warning look. Jenny pressed her lips together not to giggle. Billie had no patience with Ava's concerns over the handful of pounds she'd gained while staying at the cottage. And while Ava had largely accepted that she was done dieting and that not a single person who loved her cared a straw about the size of her hips, Ava still worried about being judged when so many guests would look at her.

Jenny understood. One didn't come to Mendocino Cove and magically lose all hang-ups. Some took a little longer than others.

"Of course, that's what we're here for." Hazel nodded. "Can I ask where the ceremony is? On a beach or inside?"

"It's in my garden," Ava said. "Overlooking the ocean, so there'll be a bit of a breeze. And later, there'll be dancing."

"Do you prefer a dress from a certain time period?"

"No." Ava hesitated. "Well, no."

"Any preference for a certain feel to the dress?"

"Um. Nothing too blushing, please, but age appropriate. And if you have any, I'd really prefer an off-white or champagne color."

Hazel nodded thoughtfully. "Let me have a look. Feel free to browse yourselves too, if you like."

Jenny brightened. "Yes, please!"

They followed Hazel deeper into the store.

The soft, sweet, barely perceptible aroma of vanilla and freshly cut ivy made her take a deep breath. Jenny liked the cozy, inviting ambiance better than the stark white and mirrors of the last store. And the samples on the mannequins were unique. This was not a store for discarded dresses nobody wanted anymore—this was a store where you brought your much-loved dress so another woman might have a chance at the happiness it brought.

Humming, Jenny started sorting through the clear bags hanging on a rack. She loved hunting for the perfect dress. Handling the gorgeous wedding materials felt so luxurious. And Ava didn't make the hunt too easy, either. Jenny's friend really wanted to get it right for her husband.

Faye, with her discerning eye, called out first. "Whoa, Jenny, look at this one."

"Mmh. Very elegant," Jenny agreed. "Let's show it to Ava."

Faye lifted the hanger off the rod. "Ava?" They went to the other side of the store, where the door of one of the two dressing rooms was closed.

Billie, a resigned look on her face, was sitting on the sofa in front of the bridal pedestal.

Faye grinned as she passed. "Dreaming of feeding pelicans, Bills? Or maybe eating lunch yourself?"

Billie only sighed.

Jenny knocked on the door. "Are you in there?"

"Yes. Give me just a moment. I'll be right out."

Jenny and Faye sat down on either side of Billie.

"She's trying out the dress she picked herself," Billie said gloomily.

Finally, the door opened. First Hazel came out, and then Ava. She was wearing a soft pink dress with a classic A-line silhouette. It had a fitted bodice, puffed sleeves, a sweetheart neckline, and a gradually flaring skirt down to her ankles.

A small, polite line between Hazel's eyes and a large one between Ava's told Jenny everything she needed to know. "It's pretty," she said diplomatically when really, she wanted to ask why on earth Ava would waste time trying on a dress like this.

"Um. No." Billie shook her head. "Sorry, Ava, puffed sleeves? Come on. You're exhausted; we all are. We should have something to eat."

"Maybe the taffeta isn't the best for the garden setting," Hazel suggested delicately.

"Or the entire eighties vibe," Billie murmured. "You'd need a sweatband instead of a veil for this one."

"But it reminds me of my wedding dress, and I thought that would be a nice touch." Ava tried to look over her shoulder to see her back. "My uncle ruined my dress when he stepped on my train and ripped the fabric. I always wished I could have saved it."

"Ava, darling, you don't want a train in the garden," Faye said reasonably. "It's not the best fabric, either. The dress is meant for an inside wedding."

Hazel threw her a grateful look.

"All right." Ava sighed. "I know. I get it. I agree. I just had to try it on because mine was so similar, but I got it out of my system. Let's carry on."

"I have a good dress for you," Faye said and stood, lifting the dress she found off her lap. "What do you think about this one, Ava?"

"I like it." Ava blinked. "I was thinking of something more shaping. But I do like it. Can I see?"

Inside the protective clear bag, the short dress hung from glittering spaghetti straps straight down to a swinging hem just below the knee.

"I like it too," Jenny said. "I like the beads. And the length should come in handy in the garden and for dancing."

"This dress is an original from the twenties." Hazel took it gently from Faye. "Good choice. I had it in mind for you too, Ava. It's a little more expensive, though. Wedding dresses from that era are hard to get, especially if they're in as pristine a condition as this one." She showed Ava the attached tag.

"I don't know." Ava hesitated. "The price is fine, and it's beautiful. That's not the problem. I love the way it looks." Longingly, she held up the dress bag to see better.

"The dress is in the famous flapper style." Hazel smiled. "It would be about your size too." She lifted the bag so Ava could see it better. "Do you want to try it on?"

"Yes." Ava looked at Jenny for help. "But I do prefer something with a defined waist. That way, I don't have to suck it in." She laughed self-consciously and put a hand to her stomach almost the same way Faye did.

"You look perfectly beautiful," Jenny said, nonplussed. "Even if you weren't—you get to eat what you like, and you get to look how you like, and also you get to wear what you like."

"Did Bruno say he thinks you gained too much weight?" Billie asked testily from the sofa and crossed her arms.

"No." Ava shook her head. "On the contrary. He likes it, which is a real surprise. All these years I tried to be skinny for him..."

Faye had to laugh. "You should see your pout, Ava. It doesn't sound like your belly bothers anyone. Are you sure you need to hold it in for your guests?"

"No," Ava said slowly. "It's probably all in my mind."

"You have my permission to *ignore* your mind," Billie growled.

Jenny patted Billie's shoulder. "Billie needs lunch soon," she mouthed, and louder, she said, "If you like how the dress looks, what's holding you back?"

Ava took the dress from Hazel. "Nothing."

"Say it again," Jenny encouraged her. "Full sentence."

"Nothing is holding me back," Ava said. She laughed and repeated her words louder and with more emphasis. "Nothing holds me back! I do what I want!"

"Finally," Billie groaned. "Now that it's out there, it won't go back in the bottle, either. Try on the dress, Ava. It is gorgeous. And I *am* hungry."

"Let's do it," Ava agreed.

"I saw a photo of this dress on the original owner," Hazel said. "She told me some stories about herself and her friends that were so interesting. They were all about liberty and independence. I've been in love with this dress ever since. You'll look stunning in it. I promise."

She held out a hand to help Ava step off the pedestal, and the two disappeared back into the changing room.

It didn't take long before they reemerged.

A small, collective gasp escaped Jenny and her friends. "Beautiful!" Jenny breathed, and Hazel nodded, a gratified expression on her face.

The dress was a soft champagne hue, and the loose fabric draped gracefully around Ava's curves. Art deco patterns of shimmering sequins, pearls, and iridescent beads danced across the fabric every time she moved.

"You look like Rose from the Titanic!" Faye whispered, her hands folded. "You're so elegant!"

Ava smiled. "I suppose my marriage did live through a shipwreck and survived." She stepped on the pedestal, the short hemline fringe shimmying with each move.

"It's really pretty," Billie admitted. "The prettiest one yet."

"It's silk, isn't it?" Jenny asked.

"Yes, it is," Hazel confirmed.

"I feel glamorous. The silk is so incredibly comfortable." Ava moved her shoulders, and the dress danced. She laughed and moved again.

"Show us the back," Faye said.

Ava twirled around. "Is it too much?"

"No, it's perfect." Jenny loved the intricate, beaded straps that braided into dainty geometrical patterns over the shoulders before meeting the fabric.

"Very alluring," Faye confirmed. "Like those modern bra tops with the pretty crisscross straps, but sophisticated. I love it."

"You won't find anything better. Take it," Billie commanded.

Ava looked at them over her shoulder. "Should I?"

"It goes with your unique house—and the fairy-tale garden setting," Jenny said. "It's a hundred percent yes from me."

"Me too." Faye gave two thumbs-up. "I really want to see it outside with the blue sea in the background. And you, dancing in it. It's mesmerizing."

"It's the perfect blend of vintage and contemporary style," Hazel said. "The past and the present." She smiled. "Back in the twenties, the original owner married against her father's wishes. She didn't have money for a wedding dress, but luckily, she had a wealthy great-aunt. When she brought me the dress a couple of weeks ago, she said that she'd had a long, happy marriage with a good man, and now she wanted her dress to bring someone else luck." Hazel cleared her throat, obviously still touched by the old lady's story. "She thought of this dress as a symbol of love, resilience, and the beauty that comes with embracing one's own journey." She reached to adjust the strap on Ava's shoulder. "You look stunning in it. It's the perfect dress for a recommitment ceremony."

Ava nodded, but then suddenly, tears welled up in her eyes as she looked at her reflection. "What happened?" she asked softly. "Not so long ago, I felt lonely and old, and like I had wasted my time in a loveless marriage. Now I feel beautiful and cherished, and like I'm on a journey of love and growth."

"Good friends and good food happened. That's your answer." Billie gathered her shopping bags and stood. "Talking about which, Ava, I'm *starving*."

"Billie!" Jenny and Faye admonished at the same time.

"So—yes?" Hazel asked, smiling at Ava.

"Absolutely," Ava said. "It's perfect."

"Applause!" Jenny called, and they all clapped their hands, glad to see their friend happy and self-confident and back home.

CHAPTER 28

The sun started to set as the ceremony came to a close. The guests stood on the bluff before a large arc draped with garlands of wildflowers, overlooking the horizon as the sun sank in a blaze of bright pink, burnished orange, and flaming red. The waves lapped against the shore, and seagulls flew overhead, calling out to each other. The only other voice was that of the officiant, who had talked about love being like the sea, ever changing but always the same, a force uniting past and present.

Ava and Bruno repeated vows of love and commitment to each other and leaned in for a tender kiss.

Audrey clapped and cheered with everyone else while music began to play in the garden.

Ava smiled at Bruno and took the hand he offered. They turned to their many friends from Seattle and Mendocino Cove, who started to hug and congratulate them.

Audrey waited her turn to hug the two, and she drifted off sideways. The people she knew were busy doing one thing or the other in preparation for the cutting of the cake and the dancing, except Billie's sons.

Louis had caught her eye a couple of times during the ceremony, and Audrey had winked back. Louis was definitely a flirt, but he was nice enough. She was planning on dancing both with him and his calmer older brother, Ben.

The only other person their age at the ceremony was Zoe. Audrey had met her briefly on one of Zoe's short visits to her parents' house in Mendocino Cove. Though there hadn't been much time to get to know each other, Audrey rather liked Zoe's open nature.

Audrey tried to spot her in the crowd. She had seen her stand beside her mom during the ceremony, but now, Zoe seemed to have disappeared. Earlier, she had been busy helping her mom get ready. To good effect, the crowd on their folding chairs in the garden had oohed and aahed over Ava's entrance, and Bruno's best man even had to hand him a tissue.

From under lowered eyelashes, Audrey had checked. The tears had been real.

Mom and her friends, all in blue dresses with drop waists and art deco accents to match Ava's, were getting the large wooden dance floor ready, igniting torches and fairy lights and candles in pretty bubble glasses. Miles, Billie's jazz musician friend, was leading his small band into catchier dance tunes.

Another collective gasp rustled through the crowd, and Audrey turned around. Zoe and a man Audrey didn't recognize were carrying a three-tier wedding cake.

So that's what Zoe had been doing—getting the cake ready. Of course, Zoe was a baker.

"Whoa," Audrey whispered. The cake's champagne-colored fondant matched Ava's dress, as did the decoration of edible pearls and off-white, artful flowers.

Jon had shown Audrey a trick or two about baking, and she could appreciate the effort and skill that had gone into the flawless execution of this towering beauty.

Now Billie clanged a teaspoon on her champagne flute and called everyone to the buffet table for the cutting of the cake. A general milling and movement toward the long tables started, and those who were still seated from the ceremony quickly joined in.

Audrey shuffled closer too, just in time to catch a glimpse of Bruno and Ava cutting the cake together and starting to hand out plates with luscious slices on them.

"Hey, Audrey."

She turned around. Behind her stood Zoe, two plates with cake in her hands. "Hi, Zoe."

"Do you want?" Zoe held out one of her two slices.

"Very much. Thanks." With a smile, Audrey took the offering. "It's the most gorgeous cake ever, Zoe. You made it, didn't you?"

Zoe nodded. "Let's go sit down somewhere? I've been so busy helping Mom and Dad and assembling the cake I haven't had a minute all day. And I'm starving."

"There are chairs over there." Audrey pointed to the edge of the dance floor, and they went and sat. Audrey tried her cake. "Mmm. This is delicious, Zoe."

"Lemon coconut," Zoe replied. "Mom wanted vanilla, but, hey. I thought I'd give her a little surprise." She smiled and tried the cake too. "Good enough," she said critically.

"It's definitely better than good enough, Zoe," Audrey said reasonably.

"I put more effort into the decoration than the cake," Zoe confided. "Thinking back, I wish I'd baked it in Seattle and brought everything on the plane instead of baking it here. Mom has a new oven, but it could barely fit the bottom tier. I had to make two to get it right."

Audrey let her plate sink. "I didn't realize, Zoe. You could have used our oven at the hotel. You could've baked the entire thing standing up in there."

Zoe gave her an amused look. "Really? Standing up?"

Audrey grinned. "All right, not that. But it is enormous. Jon sometimes bakes bread in it when he wants to make extra for friends, and I use it for my own humble cakes when the mood strikes. But it was meant for professional use, not my twenty-four cupcakes."

"Shoot, I should've gotten in touch! I forgot that you live in a hotel."

"You should visit me there sometime," Audrey suggested lightly. "How long are you staying in town?"

Zoe sighed. "Not long. They need me at the Seattle bakery where I work. I'm trying to quit, but every time I talk to my boss, another big order seems to come in, and it's all hands on deck again. I don't want to leave them hanging, you see?"

Audrey nodded. "That's nice of you. But it doesn't sound like the best long-term strategy. At least not where you are concerned. Maybe instead of giving notice, it would help to work in someone new to take over your job?"

"I actually know the perfect person," Zoe said, sounding surprised. "How did I not think of that before? I'll talk to my boss. I'm sure she'll be relieved to have a better solution than having to talk me into staying every other week."

"And later? What are you going to do next?" Audrey ate more of her cake.

"I'll move here." Zoe looked at her hands. "The guy I was dating has become a bit of a problem. I don't mind getting out of town for a while."

Audrey's eyes widened. "Is he stalking you?"

Zoe shrugged her shoulders. "Maybe he is. I'm still hoping he will just stop contacting me. I was in over my head with that relationship." She looked over her shoulder. "Don't tell my parents, okay? Mom will freak out."

"Maybe she should," Audrey murmured. "Do you feel unsafe?"

"A little bit," Zoe admitted. "But it's possible I'm being unfair and just imagining things."

Audrey bit her lip. "Why would you think you're just imagining it?" she asked. "I'm sorry. I realize it's not my place to pry. I really want you to be safe."

"I know. It's fine. To answer your question... I suppose I haven't told him to stop calling. Or, for that matter, to stop by my apartment."

"But did you break up with him?"

"Um." Zoe looked guilty. "I told him I needed some time alone to sort myself out." She cleared her throat. "Anyway. Enough about me. What about you? What are you doing?"

It sounded as if Zoe was more scared of her ex than she had admitted. But pushing did not feel right. "I have a degree in hotel management," Audrey said. "I'm fresh out of college."

"That's perfect!" Zoe exclaimed. "You have a big old hotel to get right to work!"

"Actually," Audrey said and scooped the last of the cake onto her fork, "the hotel belongs to my great-aunt. And get this." She chewed and swallowed. "This is the best cake, Zoe. And I've been in town long enough to tell a good cake from a mediocre one."

"Thank you!" Zoe smiled back. "But what did your aunt say?"

"She wants to sell the hotel," Audrey said. "Just because. I'm not even sure she needs the money."

Zoe raised a surprised eyebrow. "Then why sell? Are you on bad terms with each other?"

"I've never met her, at least not while I was old enough to remember," Audrey said and set her fork on her empty plate. "But she used to live in the hotel when her sister—my grandmother—got lost in the forest and died. From what I understand, my aunt never lived at the hotel again."

"That's too bad." Zoe also finished her cake. "Maybe the two of us should buy it off your aunt."

Audrey could tell Zoe wasn't serious, but she didn't miss the glance from her new acquaintance, either. "Maybe," she said lightly and stood. "Allegedly, Aunt Georgie will come visit us any day now. I can't wait to ask what her plans really are."

Zoe stood too, stretching her arms as best she could while holding an empty plate. "Let me know," she said. "Let me know, okay?" She started walking toward the buffet.

Audrey kept up with her. "Okay. Sure." She suddenly felt lighter. As if her future was not so uncertain after all.

Now, she had a friend who was in the same boat as her. She was no longer alone.

The sun had set, and the moon had risen. The torches were flickering cheerfully, and where neither moon nor fire illuminated the festivities that went on all around them, fairy lights twinkled romantically.

"There you two are." Louis stood up from his folding chair as they walked past them.

"Where were you?" Ben stood too, a look of relief on his face.

"There *you* are," Zoe said and smiled. "We were eating cake and talking." She pointed to their spot.

Ben looked over his shoulder and adjusted the knot of his tie. "Listen, I don't know anyone under forty here. Do you two want to join forces with us? We could have a glass of champagne."

Audrey set her and Zoe's plates on one of the bistro tables that were scattered throughout the garden and lit up by the candles in their pretty hurricane glasses. She scanned the dance floor, where most of the guests, including Mom and all her friends, were dancing, laughing and chatting and clearly having the time of their lives.

The song ended, and Miles led his little band into his version of a pop song Audrey recognized. She held out a hand, and Ben took it. "Let's dance first," she said. "And afterward, we'll have champagne. Okay?"

Louis offered his arm to Zoe, who slipped her arm under his. "I've been waiting for someone to make sense," he announced and started walking.

Laughing, Zoe looked over her shoulder at Audrey. "Don't leave me hanging," she pleaded.

Ben looked at Audrey, his dark eyes smoldering. "We could totally leave them hanging," he murmured. "You and me and the champagne—how about it? I'll tell you everything you never wanted to learn about Pomeranians' digestive troubles."

"Sounds swell." Audrey smiled. "But we're totally going to dance instead. I like this song."

"As you wish." Ben straightened, squared his shoulders, and without further ado, let go of her hand to slide his arm around Audrey's waist. She squealed in surprise and was still laughing when he whisked her off to join the dancers.

CHAPTER 29

The lights twinkled, and the music swept even the kids onto the dance floor. Faye was already breathless, half from laughing, half from dancing, and half, she figured, from being pregnant. Gabe lifted his arm; Faye swirled, laughing, when suddenly, she stumbled.

"Whoops!" Gabe caught her in his arms. Keeping her there, he swayed slowly from side to side, still dancing but allowing her to regain her balance. "Are you okay, my love?"

She smiled up at him. Never in her life would she get tired of hearing him call her his love. "Just a little dizzy."

"Dizzy without a single sip of champagne?" He smiled back. "Maybe it's time to sit down and have a drink."

"And by drink you mean..."

"Water. For you. Me, I'll have champagne." His sapphire eyes twinkled in the light of the torches. "You're the designated driver for the next eight months, mama."

"The baby's not even born, and already I'm the family chauffeur," Faye joked.

He pulled her closer and lowered his head. "Did you say family?" he murmured into her hair. "Say it again."

She smiled but didn't respond.

"Hmm." Gabe's breath brushed her cheek, as warm and reassuring as his arms.

Faye closed her eyes and rested her head on his chest.

"Then I'll say it," he murmured. "*Family.*" He pulled back just enough to see her face. "I like the sound of that. Family. My own little family."

Faye looked up at him. She had known him for such a short time. But his face was already the dearest sight to her.

After her broken engagement so many years ago, Faye had never dated seriously again. She'd had flings, and crushes, and a few one-night stands in her younger years. But her heart had always been her own. She never let herself fall in love again.

Until now.

Suddenly, love was everywhere.

Faye loved falling asleep in Gabe's arms. She loved waking up beside him. There was nothing as heart-warming as Gabe kissing her awake and handing her a cup of hot, milky tea before he went to work. The few nights where he had to stay at his own place and couldn't come over, or the nights he had to work, Faye missed him more than she'd thought possible.

For many years, she'd been perfectly content to be on her own. But no longer. Now, she wanted to be with him always.

"Our own little family," she said softly. "I like the sound of that too."

The music slowed down even more, the new rhythm releasing the dancers. The dance floor emptied of the laughing, chatting, excited crowd, who took the opportunity to drink a glass or grab a bite to eat from the luscious buffet.

Only a few couples like Ava and Bruno and Jenny and Jon hugged closer and swayed in small circles, eyes closed, lips smiling or sweetly kissing their partner. Even in the silvery moonlight, everyone could plainly see the love on their faces. Faye felt it in the air and the way the light, warm breeze caressed her skin. She felt it in the bloom of the wild roses that grew around them and the way Gabe's arms guarded her.

For a long time, Faye had felt like she lived at the edge of safety, especially when she almost lost her store and house. But that time was over. She closed her eyes, and Gabe, as if he could sense her thoughts, tenderly tightened his hold on her.

Nothing could happen to Faye now. Protective by nature, Gabe would watch out and allow not even a stumble to hurt her. She would watch out for him. He, too, needed someone to take care of him.

"Faye?" His deep voice was low. "Are you tired?"

"No." She looked up and smiled. "I love you."

He smiled back. "I thought you were asleep on your feet."

"Mmm." She held his gaze. "And you, Gabe? Do you love me?"

Gabe told her he loved her every morning and every night. But Faye would never hear it often enough.

His throat moved as if he were talking, and while no sound came from his lips, the expression in his eyes told Faye all she needed to know. She settled her head back against his chest, and for a while, they turned silently in wide, soft circles. Gabe loosened his hold. "Do you want to walk a bit, Faye? The stars are beautiful."

Despite her earlier claim, Faye was getting sleepy. It had been a long day, full of errands and tasks and last-minute decisions. Everything had gone perfectly, but now that the music had calmed, the excitement was catching up with her. "Why don't we take a starry walk tomorrow?" she whispered.

"I don't think I can wait," he murmured so low she thought he was talking to himself. Louder, he said, "Take a walk with me. Only to the bench over there."

On their next slow turn, Faye blinked at the bench. The torch beside the bench flickered in the breeze and went out, as if the sea had decided it was time for everyone to go to bed. "I don't know. There might be mosquitoes over there..." She nestled deeper into Gabe's arms. "Should we go home?"

A sigh raised and lowered his chest, and then a chuckle vibrated through it. "Faye?"

"Yes?"

"Look at me, darling."

"Let's finish this song, and then we—"

Faye blinked when Gabe let go of her. Without his warm arms, the night breeze was suddenly cool, and her slinky dress left her back bare. "What?" she asked, confused.

In the middle of the moonlit dance floor, Gabe knelt down on one knee. Faye's body realized what he was doing before her mind caught up. She gasped and covered her mouth in shock.

"Gabe?" she whispered, glancing at the dancers around them.

Jenny had noticed something unusual was happening. She and Jon came to a stop, watching with wide-eyed interest.

"Faye." Gabe's gaze was gentle but unyielding, waiting for hers.

"Yes?"

He took her hands in his and looked up into the starry night sky before beginning to speak. "Faye, this isn't exactly how I envisioned this proposal," he said softly and glanced at another couple that had stopped twirling to watch. "But I waited for this night with everything I have, and there's no way I'll wait until tomorrow." He moistened his lips. "You know I love you."

"I love you too," Faye whispered.

"I love you, and I want to make sure you know that..." His voice gave out, and he took a moment to collect himself. "No matter what life throws at us, I will always be here for you and our child."

"Oh, Gabe..." Faye blinked away a tear and tugged on his hand. "Come here."

He stood, running a trembling hand through his hair. By now, even the last pair of lovers on the dance floor had caught on to what was happening and stopped to watch.

Gabe looked around unseeingly before continuing. "I promise to love you unconditionally and protect you from all harm. To provide for our family and be a source of strength when times are tough. To listen when you need someone to talk to and laugh with you when times are good." He reached into his suit pocket and produced a small velvet box.

An expectant huff went through the onlookers. A small crowd had gathered around the dance floor.

"Will you marry me?" Gabe asked with a voice trembling as much as his hand as he opened the box to reveal the glistening diamond ring.

Faye's heart swelled with joy. She couldn't talk, but she could wrap her arms around him, burying her hands in his hair and hiding her face on his shoulder. Gabe lifted her off her feet, hugging her to him.

He closed his eyes, holding her tight. "Is that a yes?"

"Yes. A thousand times, yes. Of course I will marry you!"

The guests erupted into cheers and applause as Gabe set Faye back on her feet and slipped the ring onto her finger. Faye smiled, and he lowered his head to kiss her.

When Gabe straightened again, he exhaled a long, deep breath. "Are you still sleepy?" he whispered to her as people called out their congratulations and took pictures of the new couple, the flashlights like fireflies in the night. "Or are you finally taking that starry walk with me?"

"Starry walk, I think," Faye whispered back and laughed. She held out her hand, and in the light of the moon, the remaining torches, and the flashes from their well-wishers' phones, it sparkled and glistened like the sea herself. Ava threw them kisses as they went past, and Jenny waved, and Billie stood, open-mouthed, as Gabe put his suit jacket over Faye's shoulders and took her away from the commotion and into the velvety night.

The ocean breeze blew through their hair as they stood on the bluff, overlooking the vast ocean before them.

"You know that I'm no prize," he said in a low voice. "My job is infamous for being tough on family."

"I'll take you the way you are," she promised. "Promise to be safe, and I'll be okay."

"I'll promise to be as safe as I can," he said. "Coming home to you every night will make it worth it."

"When did you decide to ask?" Faye nestled closer. Despite the cool breeze, he was warm; he had even folded up his shirt sleeves. "I didn't expect it."

She felt him smile more than saw it, and then his other arm held her too. "I started thinking about the words I'd use the night I came into a very disorderly living room, in a forgotten hotel, and saw the most beautiful woman in the world glaring at me."

"No."

"I promised myself that I would do whatever it took to make her happy and keep her safe. And when you were so sick at the vinery—"

"You did not know I was pregnant," she protested. "*I* didn't even know!"

He kissed the top of her head. "Some of us are a little slower on the uptake than others," he teased with a smile in his voice. "That's why we have to help each other."

She laughed, too comfortable to swat him. "Well, okay, so you allegedly knew. Go on."

He chuckled. "When I thought you were pregnant with my child... I had to tell you how I felt soon. I loved you. I will love you forever."

"I love you too." Happy, Faye looked out at the stars that glistened in the sky like the ring on her finger.

"I've never loved anyone before," Gabe said after a while. "I thought I did. But it wasn't love, only attraction."

"Really?"

"Yeah." He tightened his hold on her. "Now I see that I was waiting for you. I honestly don't know what I'd have done if I'd already been married when I met you."

"Adultery?" Faye asked. "Leave everyone and everything for my precious self?"

"Probably." He chuckled. "Though I'd have taken the dog."

"Hey." She laughed, and then she leaned back a little to see his eyes and took his face in her hands. "You would do no such thing because that's not the kind of man you are."

He smiled at her.

"If you want a dog, I will give you one," she said softly. "A puppy that can grow up with Tantor and our baby."

"A puppy?" He blinked. "A puppy that can guard you and the baby when I'm at work—I like it. Pick out a big puppy."

"To scare off my friends?"

"Well, a medium pupper will do."

"I'll see what I can get." Faye smiled. "Do you want to go home?" she whispered. "I'm not tired now, but I can think of other things to do than stand around on a starry bluff." The music had picked up again, and even though the crowd was thinning, enough people took back to the dance floor.

"I can think of a whole lot of things too," Gabe murmured, his voice husky. "But before we go—may I have one dance with my fiancée?"

"I'd love to," she whispered.

He offered her his hand, and Faye took it. They danced under the moonlight in the grass and the flowers, knowing in their hearts they would always be there for each other.

When their dance ended, Faye leaned in to kiss him. As they pulled away, Gabe took her hand and said, "Let's go home, my love."

Together, they walked toward the car, ready to start their new life together. As they drove away from the house, Faye looked back at the ocean, grateful for the beautiful moment that had just happened. Their life together would not be without its challenges. But with Gabe by her side, she was ready for anything.

CHAPTER 30

J enny stepped over the flower garland on the living
room floor and set the empty salad bowl on the
inside buffet. "Hello, you two." She smiled at Ava and
Bruno, who were just coming inside.

"Thank you, Jenny. You've been wonderful. You too,
Jon." Ava extricated herself from her husband's arm.
"Go ahead, Bruno. I'll be there in a moment."

"Good night, you two. And thanks very much for your
help from me too. It was a beautiful evening." Bruno
hugged Jenny, shook Jon's hand, and then went in the
direction of the master bedroom.

"We're almost done," Jon said. "A couple more plates
and bowls left outside, that's all."

"Leave them. You don't have to clean anything," Ava
protested and took a platter from his hand to set it on
the table. "We hired a few people to help us tomorrow."

Jenny adjusted her gown and smiled at Jon. "Maybe
we should leave the happy couple to their...well, not
wedding night, but close enough."

"We should." He put an arm around Jenny's waist.

Billie came in through the sliding door, carrying two
bottles. "I think that's the last of the champagne," she

said, clamping one of the bottles under her arm and adjusting the strap of her shimmering blue halter top. "I can't believe it. We ordered so much! At least Jon went around and made sure everyone had a designated driver."

"Ava, are you okay with Faye's proposal today?" Jenny asked suddenly. "I'm sure Gabe didn't mean to pull attention away from you. In fact, I heard him trying to talk Faye into taking a walk away from the dance floor. But she didn't catch his meaning."

"I'm not only not bothered, I loved everything about it," Ava said cheerfully. "What could be better than a proposal? It was touching, wasn't it?"

Jenny nodded. "It was. I think it'd be lovely for them to get married before the baby comes. They might as well start out as an official family."

"Before or after, I'm happy for them," Billie said. "I've never seen Faye like this; she's clearly over the moon. And Gabe...well, it was just a matter of time before someone snapped him up, and I was rooting for Faye all along." Billie sighed and hitched the champagne bottle under her arm higher. "Jon, are you staying at the hotel tonight?"

"Actually..." Jon exchanged a look with Jenny, and she gave the slightest nod. They'd both noticed the effect the proposal had had on his sister.

Billie wasn't jealous of Faye's new family beginning—but maybe dejected at now being the odd one out. For decades, she and Faye had been happily single together. Now, she was best friends with three women deeply in love. It was bound to make her wonder whether she still belonged just the same as before.

"What?" Billie looked up.

"I have to get up really early tomorrow," Jon said and yawned. "I'm going to sleep at the winery." He grabbed Jenny and kissed her on the cheek. "Good night. I'll see you tomorrow."

"Goodnight." Jenny smiled. Of course Jon would have liked to come home with her—but he wanted her and Billie to talk.

"Billie, I don't feel like going to bed yet," Jenny said after Jon had slung his jacket over his shoulder and was gone. "What do you think about staying at the hotel tonight? We could have a night cap on the patio."

"Sounds good," Billie said gratefully. "I need a moment to rearrange my outlook on life now that you all hitched up. You can hold my hand and pour the champagne while I do it."

"Glad to," Jenny said. Then she went to hug Ava. "Congratulations, my friend. A fresh start and a new life that builds on the past—it's going to be wonderful. And I'm so glad to have you and Bruno live in Mendocino Cove."

"Thank you for everything." Ava hugged her back, then Billie, and then Billie and Jenny left together, leaving the married couple to enjoy the rest of their night.

"Where's Audrey?" Billie asked when they climbed into her old pickup truck. "And for that matter, where are Zoe and my boys?"

"They danced for a while, and afterward, they went to end the evening at the Mermaid Galley," Jenny reported. "Hannah and Michael took them because they wanted clam chowder and sourdough bread. And, I suspect, a break from us old fuddy-duddies."

"Speak for yourself." Billie handed Jenny her bottle to hold and started the truck.

For a while, they drove in silence. "If I'm honest, I do feel old," Billie admitted suddenly. "I'm truly happy for Faye and you and Ava. But it's like an era coming to an end."

"I know." Jenny scooted over on the bench and rested her head on her friend's shoulder. They were driving under the trees on Main Street. The canopy hid the moon, and it was dark but for the truck's headlights. The cool air streaming in through the windows smelled of night-blooming jasmine and the sea. "I know," Jenny repeated softly. "We need to find someone for you too."

Billie sighed. "There is nobody," she said, and Jenny heard her chuckle. "I'm not lonely," she added, her voice reassuringly clear. "I just don't want to be the third wheel when I hang out with the people I love most."

"Aww." Jenny smiled and straightened. "You love us?" Billie wasn't the type to declare her feelings openly.

"Of course I do." Billie flicked the blinker and turned into Forgotten.

"It's not going to happen," Jenny assured her. "We know each other too well. You're never going to feel like a third wheel because we love you too."

"I know." Billie pulled up in front of the hotel.

It was late, well after midnight, but there was light in several windows.

They sat in the truck under the old cypress tree, looking at the hotel. "Remember how I thought the hotel was haunted?" Jenny laughed.

"We still don't know it wasn't," Billie pointed out. "The heirloom armoire opening by itself, the shivers Faye got every time she passed the piano... It only stopped once you found the letters. Do you think it was your mother or your grandmother poking us in the right direction until you had what you needed?"

Jenny smiled. "I would like to think that's true," she said softly. "I would like to think they're still here, helping us along."

Billie leaned out of her truck window to look at the stars in the sky. "Mom, Dad...send me the love of my life, please," she said, and for once, she didn't sound like she was joking. "If you could let me catch a glimpse of him, I'd appreciate it." She pulled her head back in and looked at Jenny.

Jenny nodded. "Can't hurt to ask."

Billie nodded and opened her truck door. Before she could jump out, her cell phone dinged. "What the..." she murmured and checked her texts.

"What?" Jenny had already gotten out and walked around the truck to meet Billie. "Who is it?"

"My ex." Billie tucked her phone away. "Of all the people they could have sent my way, they picked my ex?" She got out and slammed her door shut. "Funny, Mom. Or Dad. Both, probably."

"What does he want?"

"He wants us all to get together. Me, him, the boys."

"Is that normal for him?" Jenny didn't know too much about Billie's failed marriage because Billie didn't like to talk about it. She was the best friend, but also the one playing her cards closest to her chest.

Billie shook her head. "We only text if the boys need something. The last time I heard from him was months ago."

"It's possible the boys told him about the party tonight," Jenny suggested. "The idea of you three being together could have prompted him to write the text."

Billie sighed. "I don't want to meet."

"Tell him that," Jenny said and pushed open the front door. It was unlocked, and the sea glass chandelier glowed brightly.

"I will. But let me tell you, it's not exactly the sign I was hoping for."

Jenny closed the door, and then she hugged her friend.

Billie was always there when anyone needed anything, always ready to give and take care of others, no questions asked, full of compassion and kindness. Not only was she the beating heart of their small group of friends, but of the entire town of Mendocino Cove. More than anyone, she deserved true love and a strong pair of arms to hold her.

"What's that for?" Billie extricated herself from the embrace. "Did you drink too much? You should have tea with honey instead of a nightcap. That would be better. You'll thank me tomorrow."

"I'm sure tomorrow will be interesting, one way or the other." Jenny smiled and waved her friend along. "Come on, Billie. Let's grab blankets and have a last glass of champagne on the beach."

Thank you for reading A Sea of Past and Present! *Read the next book in the series,* A Lighthouse of Ocean and Fog, *to stay in beautiful Mendocino Cove and continue the saga!*

BAY HARBOR BEACH SERIES

★★★★★ *"Wonderfully written story. Rumors abound in this tale of loves and secrets."*
Lose yourself in this riveting feel-good saga of old secrets and new beginnings. Best friends support each other through life's ups and downs and matters of the heart as they boil salt water taffy, browse quaint stores for swimsuits, and sample pies at the Beach Bistro!

Read the Bay Harbor Beach Series

BEACH COVE SERIES

★★★★★ *"What an awesome series! Captivated in the first sentence! Beautiful writing!"*

Maisie returns to charming Beach Cove and meets a heartwarming cast of old friends and new neighbors. The beaches are sandy and inviting, the sea is bluer than it should be, and the small town is brimming with big secrets. Together, Maisie and her sisters of the heart take turns helping each other through trials, mysteries, and matters of the heart. Get the free prequel to the series!

Read the Beach Cove Series

Mendocino Cove Series

★ ★ ★ ★ ★ *"I loved it all, the history, the mystery, the sea, the love of family and friends...!"*

A gorgeous feel-good series with wonderful characters! Four friends are taking a second chance on love and life as they start over together in the small town of Mendocino Cove. Set on the breathtakingly beautiful coast of Northern California, where the golden hills are covered in wildflowers, vineyards grow sweet grapes, and the coast is rugged and wild.

Read the Mendocino Cove Series

About the Author

Nellie Brooks writes feel-good friendship fiction for women. In her books you'll find flawed, likable characters who bake and adopt animals, gorgeous coastal settings that will make you study your tea leaves for the next vacation date, secrets that are best solved together, and happy endings until every estranged friend and distant sister is safe in the arms of her small town community.

Visit www.nelliebrooks.com to subscribe to her newsletter and hear about releases, promos, and writing news! You can also follow Nellie on Facebook and BookBub.

Made in United States
North Haven, CT
09 July 2024

54574642R00157